SPECIAL MESSAGE TO READERS

THE ULVERSCROFT FOUNDATION
(registered UK charity number 264873)

was established in 1972 to provide funds for research, diagnosis and treatment of eye diseases. Examples of major projects funded by the Ulverscroft Foundation are:-

- The Children's Eye Unit at Moorfields Eye Hospital, London
- The Ulverscroft Children's Eye Unit at Great Ormond Street Hospital for Sick Children
- Funding research into eye diseases and treatment at the Department of Ophthalmology, University of Leicester
- The Ulverscroft Vision Research Group, Institute of Child Health
- Twin operating theatres at the Western Ophthalmic Hospital, London
- The Chair of Ophthalmology at the Royal Australian College of Ophthalmologists

You can help further the work of the Foundation by making a donation or leaving a legacy. Every contribution is gratefully received. If you would like to help support the Foundation or require further information, please contact:

THE ULVERSCROFT FOUNDATION
The Green, Bradgate Road, Anstey
Leicester LE7 7FU, England
Tel: (0116) 236 4325
website: www.foundation.ulverscroft.com

UNDERCURRENT OF EVIL

After Sheila Nesbitt's father is found dead in the Thames following a visit to the Satyr Club, the most exclusive gambling parlour in town, she's determined to uncover the truth of what happened. Enlisting the help of her friend, Richard Denning, they set out to investigate what grim secrets the Satyr Club is hiding behind the suave smile of the manager, Collwell, and his sultry, seductive assistant, Lady Mercia Standard, who sets her sights on Richard. Their pursuit eventually leads them to the club's mysterious owner — 'The Old Devil'.

NORMAN FIRTH

UNDERCURRENT OF EVIL

Complete and Unabridged

LINFORD
Leicester

First published in Great Britain

First Linford Edition
published 2019

A catalogue record for this book is available
from the British Library.

ISBN 978–1–4448–4112–1

Published by
F. A. Thorpe (Publishing)
Anstey, Leicestershire

Set by Words & Graphics Ltd.
Anstey, Leicestershire
Printed and bound in Great Britain by
T. J. International Ltd., Padstow, Cornwall

This book is printed on acid-free paper

1

The Girl in the Green Hat

The girl in the green hat paused suddenly, stared across the traffic-bound road, and with a little gasp started to cross quickly, weaving her way in and out of the rushing cars and buses.

There was a taxi opposite her; and there was a man climbing into it. She reached it just as it began to move away, wrenched open the nearest door, and almost threw herself into the rear seats.

The man inside started as he recognised her, and opened his lips as if he would speak; but no sound came. He went on staring while the girl regained her breath and her composure.

She broke the silence first; her words were reproachful.

'Father — where have you been?'

He licked his lips which had suddenly become dry, and stammered a feeble and

1

surprised answer.

'I — why — I've just — just been — to the usual places, you know, Sheila. The — the club, and — and . . .'

He stopped, aware that she knew he was lying. She went on:

'But dad, it wasn't fair. A full six days, and you didn't let us hear from you or know how you were. Mother's been worried stiff, you must have known that. Did you — did you have another attack of amnesia?'

He shook his head slowly. 'No, Sheila. I can't lie anymore to you. No, I didn't.'

'Then why didn't you write us — or let us know you were going away for so long? When you left home you said you'd be back the following day. Mother was expecting to leave England tomorrow, you know that too. Did you draw the money?'

He nodded. He'd drawn the money — five thousand pounds — from his wife's account in a London bank. It was to take them out of the country to a warmer climate; it was for his own benefit. He'd come home after his Army service, retired on half pay, and a physical wreck. His doctor had warned him that if he wished to last another fifteen years, he'd have to seek a sunnier spot than Budleigh Salterton. They'd decided on a villa at Naples, and he'd gone up to draw out the last of his wife's inheritance.

He groaned aloud. The girl in the green hat glanced at him searchingly.

'Father — you — did get the money — you haven't — had it stolen, or — or anything?'

He looked back at her and there was a hopeless greyness in his face. He hadn't shaved for about three days, and his weak, stubble-covered chin looked dirty. His features, she could see, had fallen in more than ever, were drawn and miserable. He said:

'I'd better tell you, Sheila — Heaven knows what your mother is going to say and think. I'm a weak, feeble fool, I admit it, but it isn't going to help much admitting it. Sheila, your mother was willing to spend her last penny to get us over to Naples in a villa, wasn't she?'

The girl nodded.

'She didn't care about the money as

long as it meant I was going to be with you longer, as long as it meant I'd not be the useless wreck I am now.'

Again the girl nodded, but added: 'The money doesn't matter, dad. We both love you, and we need you with us. Over there you'll be a new man . . . your physical weakness will patch up in . . . '

'Don't go on, Sheila. We aren't going over there — I'm afraid. Not unless I can undo what I've done . . . '

Her voice was quite calm now; she could see how he was suffering the pangs of terrible remorse. She felt for his hand and held it, tightly. She said: 'What happened, dad?'

He passed a weary hand across his brow, said: 'You see, Sheila, I'm afraid I'm weak mentally as well as physically. I can't tell you how, but I've lost every penny of that money!'

Still she betrayed no alarm; for his sake she had steeled herself not to reproach him any further. She could see only too well that his own self-reproach was hurting far more than anything she might have said to him.

'I'm an idiot,' he continued, not meeting her eyes. 'I had a few drinks, and I met a friend of mine from the club, and . . . well, I lost the money. And it was entirely my own fault. I don't blame anyone else. But when you saw me — now — I'm on my way to try and get it back. And by God, I will! If it's humanly possible, I will!'

Now a trace of alarm crept into her tones. She breathed: 'Dad! What do you mean? How can you, if it's lost?'

He patted her hand, looked at her again.

He was proud of his daughter. She was twenty-two, tall, slim yet well formed, and beautiful. Her eyes were brown, her hair auburn, her face oval and alluring. Her clothes set off her figure to perfection. He said: 'Don't worry, dear. I'm not going to do anything which would land me in prison. I can't tell you about it — at least not yet.'

She would have liked to have pressed him for fuller details, but instead she simply said: 'All right, dad. But promise you won't do anything which might get you in trouble.'

He nodded, but it was a half-hearted nod. He said, changing the topic: 'What on earth are you doing in London late at night?'

'I was looking for you, of course. I've tried your club, and they said they hadn't seen you for five days. Where have you been, dad?'

'I'll be frank with you, Sheila. I've been so terribly upset that I've wandered round, hardly knowing what I was doing. I spent the last two nights on — on the Embankment.'

'Oh, dad,' she said, sadly. 'Why? Mother wouldn't hold what you've done against you — we can find some other way of getting to Italy. Why not come home with me now, dear?'

He was stubborn with the stubbornness of all weak persons. He shook his head emphatically, said: 'No, Sheila. I'll get back every cent of the damned money before I come home. I expect to get it tonight or tomorrow, and then I'll be back. Just tell your mother you found me, that I'm quite safe, am spending a few days with an old Army comrade, and I'll be back at Budleigh Salterton tomorrow or the next day.'

Now it was her turn to be stubborn. Decidedly she said: 'Dad, if you won't come home with me, I'm coming with you. I mean that.'

'But you can't, Sheila. I'm going to a Mayfair club. A very private affair — and ladies aren't allowed.'

'I don't care. I'll wait outside . . . '

'But I may have to stay the night . . . '

'I'll still wait outside.'

He sighed. And she said: 'Now don't argue, dad. I'm not going to lose you again. Hadn't you better get a wash and brush up before you pop in at this very exclusive club?'

He looked down at his baggy trousers, which bore visible traces of his sleeping out nights. He fingered his stubbly chin.

Then he laughed, suddenly, said harshly: 'No, I'm damned if I will! That swine brought me to this state, so let him see me in it, and then perhaps he will realise that I mean what I say.'

They were approaching a long, shadowy street in the Mayfair district now,

7

and suddenly the cab pulled up before a gloomy driveway. The cabby said: 'This 'ere the spot you wants, guv'nor?'

'The Satyr Club?'

'Says so on the gates,' replied the driver.

'Good.'

He stepped out, and Sheila followed him. He fumbled in his pocket and scraped together a few shillings in small change, which he handed to the driver. The cab whirled away down the street, and he turned to his daughter again, who was looking curiously along the dark drive to the doors of a large, private house.

'Please, Sheila, be sensible. Oh, I know you're thinking I might not keep my word and come back tomorrow. But I promise you . . .'

'No. I'm waiting here, dad. As long as you stay inside there.'

'If you were ten years younger I'd take you across my knee and spank you,' he said resignedly. 'But as it is . . . oh, I don't expect you being along can make any difference. Come on.'

He walked along the drive and she kept

close by his side. There was something as evil as its name about the look of the club. She didn't like the atmosphere which clung around it, and the line of modern, rakish cars which were lined up along the drive did little to dispel her feeling that there was something wrong about the place.

And then he was knocking at the door with an immense knocker which was cast in the shape of a demon. The door opened at once, and a white coated steward peered at them.

He said: 'Oh, good evening, sir. Glad to see you've called on us again.'

Major Nesbitt pushed his way inside, drawing Sheila after him. He said, rather grimly: 'I have called again, James. But not for the same purpose. I wish to see Collwell.'

'Mr. Collwell is rather busy at present, sir,' said the servant, placing unmistakable emphasis on the MR.

'He'll see me just the same,' snapped Nesbitt. 'Be good enough to give him this note, will you?'

He handed the steward an envelope,

sealed. The steward took it, looked again at the Major, then nodded and flitted silently away.

Major Nesbitt waited impatiently. He was in a bad, nervous state, and his well-kept hands were almost crushing the cigarette he had lit to soothe himself. He started as a voice spoke just behind him, and spun round to face a tall, dark man, in immaculate dress, who had just walked along the passage towards them.

'You wished to see me?' he asked.

Nesbitt nodded. 'I do. Collwell, I have a proposition to talk over with you — you read my note?'

'With considerable interest. You appear to be a very poor loser, Major. I thought the Army taught you better than that?'

'There was nothing honest about the way I lost that money, and you know it.'

'But Major, others have lost heavily and not complained . . . '

'I was a fool, and the money was not mine to lose anyway. You've seen the note, and you know what I want. What's your answer?'

Collwell smoothed back his crinkly

black hair, smiled, said: 'You know, Major, I'm not the head of this thing. I should have to speak to the person who is, and that will take time.'

'How much time?'

'Oh, a few days — perhaps I might rush it and let you know by tomorrow, say.'

Nesbitt nodded. 'Very well. I'll give you until tomorrow at eight. I'm not playing games, Collwell. I mean every word of what I said in that note.'

'Of course you do, Major. Believe me, I understand how you feel about it. I am in complete sympathy with you, also. But I have my job to do, you know, and I merely follow instructions. Perhaps you would like to take a room here at the club for tonight, then should I receive a reply before tomorrow evening, I can let you have the money at once and the matter will be settled?'

'You have a vacant room?'

'Several.'

'Perhaps you also have one for my daughter?'

Collwell glanced for the first time at Sheila, who had been standing by, unable

11

to make head or tail of the conversation. As his eyes travelled along her figure, he smiled greasily, said: 'I really would like to find your daughter a room, Major, but, I regret, it is not possible. You know the rules of this establishment. The regular members would be sure to complain if a woman were admitted . . . '

'I know how it is. I didn't think you could manage it. Never mind, Collwell, we'll find a hotel . . . '

'Wait a minute,' the dark man said, somewhat hastily. 'Perhaps, if Miss Nesbitt kept to her room until you are ready to leave, we may be able to fix her up with something.'

He motioned to a uniformed page who hurried forward.

'Take Major and Miss Nesbitt up to twenty-four and twenty-six,' he told him.

Major Nesbitt said: 'Thank you. And don't forget, Collwell, I expect to hear from you definitely by eight tomorrow night.'

'I think, possibly, you'll hear before then,' smiled Collwell, and there was something in his tone which made Sheila shudder with sudden apprehension.

They were taken up in a noiseless lift, down a long corridor with a thick, soft carpet. The whole atmosphere of the Satyr Club was discreet and silent; and yet there was an air of menace about the place which she could not define.

She left her father at the door of twenty-four. He kissed her goodnight, an unusual thing for him. He said: 'Everything's all right, dear. Don't worry, get a good night's sleep. Evidently Collwell is going to pay up. I thought he would. Tomorrow we'll go home again, and your mother need never know anything about all this. By the way — you'd better lock your door.'

He went into his room, and she walked along to twenty-six. She noted, at the far end of the passage, a wide, green baize covered door, and wondered what was behind it, idly — possibly servants' quarters. Her room was modern and comfortable, and she undressed for bed. Recalling her father's last words, she crossed to lock the door, but there was no key. She pulled it, to get the key from the other side if it was there — and found — the door was *locked* from the outside!

2

Illusion

Locked!

She didn't become immediately pan-
icky; she went to the bed, sat down, and
thought it over. Why was that door
locked? What reason could anyone have
for wanting to confine her to her room?

She noticed a small bell push let into
the wall beside the bed, and she stabbed
at it viciously with her finger, kept it
there, so that if the bell worked it must be
playing an incessant tune somewhere
below stairs.

The door opened abruptly, and the
white coated James came in. He moved
noiselessly towards her, stood a few feet
away in a deferential attitude.

'Yes, Miss?'

She got up angrily; then, noticing his
eyes upon her figure which was covered
only by a short underskirt, she hopped

into the bed and drew the clothes over the tautness of the silk where it concealed her firm, rounded breasts.

His smile was oily and repulsive; she was covered now, but still felt as if his eyes were tiny hands, searching, exploring her. She shuddered and spoke sharply: 'Who locked this door?'

'Door, Miss?'

'I said *door*. I want to know who locked it — and why?'

He looked blank, said: 'I don't understand, Miss. If it was locked you must have locked it yourself. Who else would?'

'How could I lock it when the key isn't here?' she demanded, almost angrily.

At this he looked surprised, peered at the keyhole, then said: 'Oh, I see. The key has gone. I'm sorry, usually it is here in the keyhole, but with the room not being in use the maids must have removed it.'

'But the door was locked I tell you, and the page boy opened it with a key. Why did he lock it after him?'

'He didn't Miss. His key fits all the room doors. And the doors themselves

16

are automatic. They lock when they are closed, and can't be re-opened without the key. I will bring you a key for this door if you wish it.'

'Please do.'

'Perhaps you would also like a little something to drink? Wine, or a softer beverage?'

She considered, and began to realise how thirsty she was. She said: 'I should like a little tea, if it isn't too much bother.'

'No bother at all. I'll bring it along for you with the key.'

While he was gone she was trying to remember something. There was some fact, something he had done or said, *or done and said*, which didn't ring true. She knew there was something incongruous about his explanation of the self-locking doors, but she couldn't remember just what it had been.

He was back again before she had made any headway, bearing a silver tea-service, which he laid beside her. He handed her a thin key and she slid it beneath the pillow.

'Thank you.'

17

'If you require anything more, please ring,' he told her, once more eyeing the outlines of her figure beneath the sheets; then he withdrew to the door, bowed to her, and went out.

She poured the tea thoughtfully, sugared, and sipped. It was delicious, and she finished her first and poured a second cup. She was halfway through this when she remembered the thing he had said which hadn't fitted in. She was annoyed with herself for not mentioning it while he'd been there — annoyed because her wits hadn't been acute enough to detect the flaw in the story. She took the key from beneath her pillow, crossed to the door. She staggered slightly, feeling strangely dizzy. She shook the sensation off and turned the handle. Tried the key in the door, which was still locked.

It didn't fit!

He could have made a mistake and given her the wrong key. But she knew he hadn't because of the fact she had so suddenly, and belatedly remembered.

He had said the doors were *self-locking*, and that the key had been removed — he had told her the door could not be opened *without the key*, once closed! And yet, when she had rung for him, he had *opened the door himself!*

Of course, he may have had a master key. Yet she didn't think that was the explanation. But if she was to be kept prisoner in this room, why had he come at all? The sudden, unaccountable dizziness gripped her again, she felt her head swimming hazily, felt the room whirling about her.

The tea! That was it. The tea had been drugged to prevent her making an outcry!

She began to stagger weakly to the wall which connected with the room her father had. She wondered what it was all about and if he were in the same plight. She must hammer on the wall and let him know there was something very wrong in this place.

She was almost there, hands raised to thump, when her knees buckled under her, and she fell helplessly, full length on the soft carpet. She tried to get up, but it was useless. The more she moved the more her head whirled.

Faint and dizzy she lay there, and gradually the consciousness ebbed from her brain, leaving a complete blank. Her eyes were closed, her breathing heavy . . . she slept a drugged sleep.

★   ★   ★

It was a terrifying sleep, too; whatever had been put into the tea she had drunk, caused her to dream strange, nightmarish dreams. Gargoyles and monsters patronised her subconscious, weird, Pan-like figures roamed the mazes of her mind, and imps and ogres thronged in a mad constellation in the netherworld in which her brain roamed.

So that, restless and afraid, she writhed and wriggled and moaned.

Then there came towards her, hazily, a group of demons from the bottomless pits of Hell itself. Gibbering and glowering they moved upon her. In her dreams she was naked, and as their clutching talons reached out, she threw her arms across her body in a vain effort to protect her firm flesh from their obscene eyes. They chuckled all the more and pawed and mauled her with lascivious fingers.

She felt herself being draped in something, felt their evil hands on her again as they picked her up and bore her off into darkness, to what foul orgy she could only guess.

Wherever they were taking her it was cold; she felt the chill penetrate her garments, and shivered.

Then suddenly she was alone again, and her tortured mind sank into entire forgetfulness . . .

She woke freezing cold; for a moment she wondered if she was still dreaming, for she was lying on bare stones, in the pale glimmer of dawn, fully dressed in her own clothing.

She crawled to her feet, shakily; and a glance round told her this was no dream.

She was on the Embankment up near the wall!

The city had not yet come to life; far in the distance the clatter of a milk-roundsman made itself heard, and nearer at hand the sibilant hiss of the river passing beneath the bridge she was near.

But it was real enough; she strove to recall how and why she had come here — who had brought her. She seemed to remember, very dimly, a club called 'The Satyr Club.' But had that been part of her dream? Or . . . had it really happened?

She began to walk, trying to puzzle out how she had come there. And as she walked, details of the previous night filtered through to her, and gradually she pieced together the jigsaw, selecting fact from fantasy and welding each piece into a composite whole. But it was hard.

How much had really happened, and how much was a part of her nocturnal imaginings, she was uncertain. She remembered she had been looking for her father — and had found him. She had gone to some private club with him; he had been in trouble.

They had taken rooms, and she had taken tea, and then . . . what had happened after that?

At last she realised that her dream of gargoyles carrying her off had been inspired through fact. Someone had dressed her during her sleep, had brought her away and laid her here, on the Embankment. Why had they done that?

The Satyr Club must be tied up in it all somewhere. That must be the name of the club she had gone to last night — or had it been last night? How long had she been drugged? She found an early taxi just going out for the day's work. She was thankful they hadn't taken her bag or her money, and she ordered the driver to drive her to 'The Satyr Club.' He didn't know it, hadn't heard of it, and she realised how hopeless it was going to be looking for it.

Nevertheless she told him to drive round the quieter parts of Mayfair, and she herself kept her eyes open. It was two hours and more before they found it; but the name was on the gate, and the place itself she now remembered. She paid off the driver and walked up the drive.

The place looked different in daylight. It was now stately, sedate, none of the atmosphere she had felt about it on the previous night. But the grinning, demoniacal features which constituted the handle of the door knocker sent a shudder through her again.

She knocked.

It was the inevitable James who opened the door to her; and seeing him again brought the whole thing back with unusual clarity. She said: 'I wish to see my father!'

He raised his eyebrows, bewilderedly. He said: 'I beg your pardon, Miss?'

'My father, Major Nesbitt,' she repeated, angrily.

He frowned thoughtfully, as if trying to remember something.

'There is no one of that name amongst our guests,' he told her at last.

She almost staggered. She could hardly believe he was going to deny knowing her father — he had so obviously recognised him the night before.

She said: 'But — but surely you remember me? I came here last night — with — with my father. I — I had a room . . .'

He smiled, said: 'You must be mistaken, Miss. Ladies are not permitted in this establishment. And personally I have never seen you before.'

'You — you're lying! I know you are! Why, you brought up my tea last night

— before — before I lost consciousness.'

'Lost consciousness, Miss?'

She decided not to waste any more time on him. She said: 'May I speak to Mr. Collwell? I suppose you'll deny knowing *him*?'

'Not at all, Miss. But I'm uncertain as to whether he can see you at the moment. May I ask the nature of your business here?'

'You may tell him that unless he sees me I am going at once to the police.'

James smiled a sinister smile. He walked soft-footedly down the passage . . .

With the advent of Collwell she knew more certainly than ever that she was making no mistake. It *had* happened. She had been here, and she had been drugged. And — what had happened to her father?

Collwell, as smooth and oily as he had been the previous night, rubbed his hands and said, deprecatingly: 'What can I do for you, Miss?'

'I'm looking for Major Nesbitt — and please don't try to say you don't know him. There's something very funny about this place, and unless you take me to him at once I'll go immediately to the police!'

'But I assure you . . . ' he began.

She cut in; she was becoming angry and bewildered. What could they hope to gain by all this subterfuge? She snapped: 'Please take me to my father's room, Mr. Collwell.'

He shrugged. 'I haven't the remotest idea of what you are talking about,' he said. 'I don't know you and I don't know any Major Nesbitt, and — ' here he peered at her keenly, 'and,' he went, on, 'I would advise you to stop taking drugs, young lady!'

'How — how *dare* you . . . you know very well . . . '

'I know only that your eyes and the pupils show unmistakable traces of the drug habit . . . I know only that you have come here and caused a considerable disturbance.'

'But my father — I can show you the very room I had, the room he had . . . '

He said: 'If it will set your mind at rest to show me, you may do so.'

Without a word she turned on her heel,

walked up the stairs, with him following closely. She trod along the passage, over the same thick carpet she remembered; stopped outside twenty-four. She said: 'This was the room my father had,' and she knocked at it.

Collwell betrayed no alarm, not even when the door opened.

A man with the appearance of a business man looked out.

He said: 'Yes?'

She was dumbfounded, unable to speak. Collwell stepped forward.

'This young lady is convinced her father is here. Are you he, sir?'

'By Gad, no, but I'd rather like to be,' chuckled the stout one, with a keen look at her trim figure.

'You see?' said Collwell.

She stuttered: 'But last night — I saw him come in here only last night, I swear I did.'

The fat man said, puzzledly: 'Well, I'm damned if I did, m'dear, and I've been here for the best part of eight days now. And I've never been out after six at night, so if your father was here he must have been invisible, what?' and he let out a gush of laughter which trembled his three chins against his starched collar.

Collwell smiled: 'Thank you, sir. I hope we haven't disturbed you too much?'

'Not at all, not at all. Glad to help. Any time. Especially for such a charming young lady. I hope you find your father, m'dear, I really do.'

The door shut behind him, leaving her staring hopelessly at the blank woodwork. Collwell waited patiently.

At last she walked along to twenty-six, found the door locked. She rapped there, waited. Collwell said: 'May I ask how many more of my guests you intend to disturb with your insane fixation?'

She didn't answer him, was staring at the languid, red-haired beauty who had opened the door. She recognised the girl's features from the photographs she had seen in the *Tatler* and *Sketch* fashionable papers. 'Lady Mercia Standard and friend,' or 'Lady Standard with her championship dogs,' or 'Lady Mercia Standard at the fashionable Terrapin Night Club,' and so on.

'Hello!' drawled Lady Standard, pulling the flimsy negligee she was wearing across her swelling bosom. 'What's all this?'

Again Sheila couldn't find words to speak. Collwell stepped into the silence, said: 'This young lady is suffering from the delusion that her father spent last night in one of these rooms, Mercia. I hope it wasn't yours?'

'Mine? Oh, I say, I rather wish he had; absolutely. I'd have enjoyed that, rather. But I'm afraid he didn't, or I'd have known about it. I can generally smell a male from a distance of three to four miles, and five on a clear day; definitely.'

'It wasn't my father who had this room,' explained Sheila. 'It was myself . . . '

'You did? Rather fascinating, that. Did we sleep well?'

'You know quite well you weren't here,' said Sheila, desperately. 'I was here alone.'

Lady Standard raised quizzical eyebrows and peered at Collwell.

'What is this, Colly? A joke? Or am I the one who's mad? You know perfectly well I retired early with a headache, and this door wasn't opened until breakfast

29

time this morning. So what's the big idea of getting this young lady to say she spent the night here? You aren't trying to persuade me I spent it elsewhere, are you? Why, you know dam' well I spent it here, Colly.'

He said hurriedly: 'It isn't any of my doing, Mercia. This girl simply came here claiming her father had a room here . . . and she also. How she makes that out when she obviously didn't spend the night here at all I don't know, but she does.'

'I *did*,' cried Sheila. 'I'm sure of it. I — I spent it *here*, I tell you. I was given some drugged tea . . . '

'I can see *that*,' assented Lady Standard, peering at her. 'You really ought to hold yourself under control until the effects have worn off.'

'I didn't *take* it, and I'm perfectly all right now.'

'How do you mean, you didn't take it?'

'I mean *voluntarily*. It was put in the tea. James brought it up for me, you see, and I — I — well, afterwards I lost consciousness and dreamed . . . '

'You're still dreaming, my child,' smiled Lady Standard. 'If I were you I'd forget it all; absolutely. Of course, dreams induced by drugs always seem real enough — but I think you'll find that there wasn't any reality in your dreams. Now, I have rather a beastly headache, and I must grab an atom of shut eye before I go riding; absolutely. So if you'll forgive me . . . '

And she withdrew gracefully into the room.

Sheila wasn't beaten yet though; she whirled on Collwell with an accusing stare. 'You said ladies weren't admitted to this club?'

'Quite true. But whatever gave you the idea that Mercia is a lady, my dear? She is, but in title only. Otherwise she's a very particular friend of mine, if you understand me. That's why she often stays here . . . have you any objection?'

She was beginning to wonder if it had been all a bad dream. Had she really found her father and gone to this place with him, or had she merely imagined the whole thing? If only her head would stop spinning so maddeningly, she might be able to get things into their proper perspective. But it wouldn't, and she didn't. Slowly, followed by the grinning Collwell, who seemed to pity her condition, she went down the stairs. At the bottom she found the page boy who had taken her to her room; and his blank stare of unrecognition persuaded her not to tax him with having seen her before. Collwell showed her out!

3

The Man in the Grey Trilby

'I see, Miss,' nodded the desk Sergeant. He motioned to a lean constable who was busily cleaning the station windows. He said: 'George, take this young woman along with you and listen to what she has to say. Then investigate it, will you?'

George sighed, put down the wash-leather and wriggled into his tunic. Then they left the station, Sheila unreeling her story to him as they went. He seemed a bit dubious, and kept glancing at her worn and weary face, and her bedraggled clothing. But eventually they reached the Satyr Club, and were admitted.

Collwell came almost immediately, suave and smiling. His eyebrows went up as he saw the constable and Sheila, and he said: 'Really, constable, this is intoler- able. This young woman is fast becoming a public nuisance.'

'That may be, sir,' agreed the constable. 'But we 'ave to investigate her story.'

'Oh, I'm not blaming you — you have your job to do. But she has already disturbed my guests once today, and since they pay well for privacy and seclusion, it's a little hard, don't you think?'

'I expect it is, sir. But this young lady's story . . . '

'Of course. She claims to have spent the night here, doesn't she? And she has also mislaid her father? Oh, well, I can see I'll just have to let you speak to the steward, the page, and the two guests who occupied the rooms she claims herself and her father used. Come along with me, will you?'

They went upstairs; it was the procedure of the morning all over again, and as they progressed the constable's features became more and more embarrassed. The steward, James, denied any knowledge of her before that morning, as did the page boy. The two guests confirmed their earlier remarks.

And then Collwell took the policeman aside, and said: 'I don't like to point this out, constable, but you can see for yourself that the lady has been taking drugs. Whether she is an addict or not I'm uncertain, but her eyes indicate she has taken a liberal helping only recently. Probably all this springs from a mind muddled by drugs — but you can see for yourself there is no truth in her statement.'

'I can see that, sir,' nodded the constable. 'And I'm sorry to 'ave troubled you. I'll take her back to the station, and most likely the Sergeant'll have a few words to say to her. I don't think she'll bother you again.'

They returned to the station, and the Sergeant did have a few words to say on hearing his subordinate's story.

'Now look here, young lady,' he told her severely. 'I don't know your purpose in making all these accusations, but it's got to stop. You say you were drugged . . . ?'

'I was,' she exclaimed wildly. 'I swear I was.'

'Well, I put it to you that you wasn't — I put it to you that you took the drug yourself, and that you're still under the influence of it. I've looked your father's case up. He was reported missing from his home two days ago, and so far he hasn't been found. We'll find him in time, don't fear, but not if you're going to go round London making a fool of yourself.'

'You don't believe a word of my story?' she said, dully.

'How can I? You've got too many witnesses against you and none for you. Best thing you can do is go home and take things easy for a bit. And about these drugs — I'd advise you not to take any more, or you'll find yourself in trouble if we catch you at it. Now off you go, and if you bother the Satyr Club again we'll have to run you in as a public nuisance. On top of that the manager may prefer charges against you, then where would you be? My advice to you is to forget all about it, see? And don't let us be having any more complaints about you.'

Without answering she walked slowly from the station. What was the use of trying to convince them she was right? Collwell had played his hand too well for there to be any finger of suspicion left pointing in his direction.

But her father? What could have happened to him? What was the hold he had over Collwell that had caused him to vanish like he had? Why did he think Collwell would pay him money?

They were questions she found herself quite unable to answer. She felt tired now, and after having a cup of coffee in a café, she went into a news theatre, and sat there thinking, not even noticing the films which were showing. She sat there for three complete performances; and when she emerged her mind was made up. She could not go home and leave things as they were; any further appeal to the police would bring trouble for her; but somehow she had to find more out about the whole thing. She would have to work alone, and take her chances.

Having made that decision, she entered a post office just before closing time, and drafted out a wire. It read:

'MOTHER — AM STAYING IN LONDON UNTIL I FIND DAD STOP WILL WRITE YOU SOON — LOVE SHEILA.'

She handed it in and left the post office again. The next step was to return to her hotel room and get into some more presentable clothing. She took a taxi, paying no heed to her rapidly dwindling supply of money. It decanted her at the hotel entrance, and she went in.

She felt a great deal better for a change and wash; and after she had forced herself to eat a little, she felt equal to deciding what was to be done first of all. That was rather an awkward task — she couldn't think where she might get a clue to work on. The only plan which suggested itself was for her to hang about the grounds of the Satyr Club until something happened.

Accordingly she donned her coat and hat and went out. She walked as far as the main road, and bought a newspaper from the boy on the corner there. While she waited for a bus, she opened it and read.

There was a column which caught her eye; it began halfway down the page, and ended above an advertisement. It wasn't a big splash; but it made her clutch her head in sudden dizziness, and wrenched a little cry from her bloodless lips!

BODY IN THAMES

'Late this morning the body of an unshaven, well-dressed man was picked up by river police in the Thames. Possessions in his pockets indicate that he was a Major Nesbitt of Budleigh Salterton, and was retired after long service abroad. Major Nesbitt, we learn, has been missing for some days, and when found he was in an extremely disreputable state. Pathologists find he had been drinking heavily, and his blood contained a large percentage of alcohol. It is believed that the Major must have walked into the river while under the influence of drink.'

That was the extent of the report; but it was enough to make Sheila reel and hold onto a lamp-post for support. Her mother! Her mother must already have been informed! How would she be taking it?

She fought her way through the surging crowds to a 'phone box. There was an exasperating delay while an old lady

39

fumbled with two halfpennies which she was trying to insert in the penny slot. Then a further wait while she gabbled unceasingly to some other old dear at the other end of the line. Eventually she laid down the 'phone, apparently cut off, and came out.

'Disgusting, isn't it,' she snapped to Sheila. 'Two-pence for three minutes! There ought to be a law against it, that there ought.'

She hobbled off, and Sheila almost threw herself in the box, and with fumbling fingers drove two coins into the slot.

'Trunks, please,' she said, voice trembling. 'I wish to make a call to Budleigh Salterton,' she told the trunks operator. 'Chase 2248.'

'Ayum sorray, theyah will be a delay of several owas,' said the operator.

'But, please — it's urgent . . . '

'Ayum sorray — if you'll give me youah nember Ia'll call yow back.'

Listlessly she put down the 'phone; she couldn't hang round a public booth waiting for a return call. She walked out into the street again, dazedly, hardly knowing where she was going or what she was going to do . . . she began to cross the road . . .

There was a harsh scream of hastily applied brakes; the driver wrenched his wheel furiously, but the swerve wasn't in time. The nearside mudguard struck her a blow across the side and she was thrown violently onto the roadway.

A man in a grey trilby jumped from the car and hurried over; most of the passersby had not yet realised what had happened. They were still standing with open mouths, unable to marshal their thoughts and go to the aid of the girl in the green hat, who lay still and senseless in the roadway, with the car wheels not a foot from her slender body. It had happened too suddenly for even a shout of warning.

The man in the grey trilby bent over the girl; he was young and dark-haired, with a pleasant face and a mouth which could crinkle with laughter easily. But now his mouth was set and worried; his eyes were compassionate as he gazed down and made a hasty examination of the victim.

He raised her head on his arm, forked in his back pocket and produced a flask of whisky which he touched to her lips. She came round almost at once.

'I'm dreadfully sorry,' he told her. 'Are you hurt badly?'

She sat up easily enough, then, with his help, stood up. She said: 'No, I seem to be alright. It wasn't your fault anyway. I should have looked where I was going.'

'Nothing broken?'

'No,' she said, almost whispering. 'Just — just a little bruised, that's all.'

'Is the young lady 'urt bad, sir?' asked the constable who had come along, producing his note book officiously.

'I don't think so,' replied the man in the grey trilby. 'No, I fancy she'll be all right, officer.'

'Mmm. Well, I'll have to take details, you know. Case anything do go wrong like. 'Ow did it all 'appen?'

They told him and he made copious notes, finally snapping his book shut with a flourish. Then he said: 'D'you think you're fit to go 'ome, then, Miss?'

'Yes, thank you.'

'No, wait a minute,' said the young man. 'I'll take her to my place for a shot of brandy. She looks a bit white.'

'I — I can't. I have a very important 'phone call to make.'

'Then you can make it from my flat. In you get.'

She allowed herself to be handed into the car; she had to make the call, and his place was as good as any. He climbed in after her and the car shot through the traffic towards his apartments.

They were quite luxurious, but strictly bachelor. He made her comfortable on the settee with a strong brandy, and while she sipped it he booked her call to Budleigh Salterton.

There was an hour's delay; and this he spent talking to her.

It was easy to see how worried, how upset she was. And gradually, little by little, he drew the facts out of her. She had wanted someone to confide in, someone who would be sympathetic towards her. And in Richard Glenning

43

she found someone!

He heard her out sympathetically, and at last she said: 'I know what you're thinking. You're thinking exactly the same as the police thought. That I'd been taking drugs and didn't know what I was talking about!'

'You're wrong,' he told her seriously. 'I hadn't thought that at all. I believe you — in the first place you aren't the person to take drugs, I can tell that easily enough. In the second place I know a bit more about the Satyr Club than the police do. You see, I go there quite often. I've met Collwell — and I don't like him.'

'You go there?' she asked.

'Very often. I happen to have a decent private income and very little to spend it on. I go to the Satyr because it happens to be the most exclusive gambling parlour in town. The gambling premises are behind the main portion, and separated by a sound proof door. That, I imagine, is what your father was driving at when he demanded money from Collwell. I thought Collwell actually owned the place, but it may be possible someone else is behind him.'

'Then — then you think father lost the money gambling, and then tried to regain it by threatening Collwell with exposure?'

He nodded. 'That seems the only reasonable assumption. And Collwell therefore had your father removed, and you were placed in such a position that your story was discredited. It's a wonder he didn't kill you also, but perhaps he thought that the simultaneous deaths of both father and daughter might create a little too much unpleasantness. Yes, I feel sure that he stuffed your father with drink, then had him drowned.'

'Then — if we went to the police . . . ?'

'Wouldn't help. Collwell could have the gambling rooms turned into select dining rooms before they could get at him. And we've no proof that he murdered your father, or drugged you.'

'But what can we do?'

He frowned, then said: 'The best plan is not to rush things. You say you're determined to make Collwell pay for what he's done. I agree with you, and I sincerely want to help. But we can't do anything for the moment. I have the right

45

of entry into the gambling rooms, and they don't know I'm in league with you. Now suppose I took a room at the Satyr, kept my ears open, and kept a close watch on Lady Standard and this fat man you referred to? If I played my cards right I might find out quite a lot.'

'And what could I do?'

He thought for a moment. 'Well, on the whole, I think your place is beside your mother now. If, as you say, she loved your father so much, she is sure to be worried out of her senses. She'll need someone by her, someone she can turn to, and release her emotions with. That person must be you.'

'You think I ought to go home?'

'I do. While you're gone I'll see what I can do this end. When I find anything important out I'll write to you and if you like you can come up.'

Involuntarily she touched his hand, said: 'It's awfully good of you, Mister Glenning.'

'Forget it. Give me something useful to do for a change. And my name's only Glenning to my acquaintances — to my friends I'm known as Dick.'

He studied her delicate, appealing features over the brim of his glass. She was so young and so unwise to the ways of London and particularly Mayfair, to be mixed up in a mess like this. Alone she was sure to run into trouble — and he didn't want her to.

Funny, that, because up to now he hadn't cared much about women.

She was unusual, because she exercised a strong appeal for him, even worried, strained and bedraggled as she now was.

She was almost too worried to notice him; but she liked the strong line of his features, the tiny twist to his lips, and the lean jaws, which led to a determined chin. She knew that if anyone could help, he could, and she was more thankful than she liked to admit even to herself for his presence.

The telephone cut across her thoughts: he said: 'This'll be your call, Sheila.'

She took it; it wasn't her mother; it was the family doctor. She was only half aware of his long preambling remarks about being brave, and nerving herself. From it all she gathered only one item: 'Your mother collapsed and died of heart failure when she heard!'

4

A Night at the Satyr

Richard Glenning permitted his keen eyes to range round the crowded gambling rooms at the rear of the Satyr. Big business men jostled big time gamblers; Dukes and Viscounts rubbed elbows with stage and screen actors; crooked financiers trod on the toes of thieves and cut-throats. But all were supreme of their kind. All were notable in their own circle; and all were decorous and well-dressed here at the Satyr.

Women were not admitted to the hotel portion of the club; but here and there were almost as many women as men. They leaned over the tables, faces flushed and excited, low cut dresses falling off their breasts as their eyes followed the little spinning ball on its travels.

For the main part they were young; few men cared to bring their wives or daughters to the Satyr Club; but it was an ideal place to bring your mistress.

Richard's eyes rested on a tall, red-haired beauty in a daring gown. She was smoking a cigarette in an affectedly long holder, and casually watching play at one of the larger tables. He knew her as Lady Standard, and hitherto had displayed little interest in her. She was always round the Satyr gaming tables. But now he had reason for wishing to make her acquaintance.

He crossed ever casually and took up a position behind her. She wasn't playing herself, but was urging the straw-haired, long-nosed young ass in front of her to make desperate bets.

'Oh, come on, Oswald, you old dear,' she laughed, in her throaty voice. 'You aren't throwing it up now, are you? Why, good heavens, man, you can't afford to lose two thousand in two nights. You'll have to get some of it back; definitely.'

The young man fidgeted, said: 'It's all very well, Lady Mercia, but I daren't lose any more.'

'Don't be so essentially silly,' she

drawled, puffing smoke into his face. 'Try eighteen. I know the run of these tables — it's absolutely bound to come up this time, old thing. Do try it, Ossy.'

He grunted, and with a sudden desperate movement, pushed a thousand pounds worth of chips onto eighteen. The ball bounced, the wheel spun; slower; the ball clicked finally into nineteen.

'How dashed odd,' smiled Lady Standard. 'I could have sworn it would be eighteen. Never mind old thing, you're only a mere one out. Try again.'

The young man stood up; his eyes were frightened, as if he had done something he could never undo. He mumbled: 'I — I can't. That was — was my last penny. I — '

He suddenly turned, his eyes red; obviously he felt sorry for himself, and realised what a fool he had been. He hurried away, and Lady Standard gazed contemptuously after him.

A voice by her elbow said softly: 'Why not try it yourself instead of encouraging young fools to?'

She turned round slowly, her long

lashes veiling her eyes. She looked at the keen faced young man beside her, and deliberately blew smoke into his face. His eyes never blinked.

He continued to stare at her, challengingly.

'I fancy I've seen you before here, haven't I?' she mused, and he nodded. She went on: 'We haven't been introduced, or have we?'

'If we have you weren't impressive enough for me to remember,' he told her insolently. 'My name's Glenning — Richard Glenning.'

'Really? And mine's Lady Standard, Mercia of that clan. What were you saying previously?'

'I wondered if you yourself had the nerve to gamble the amount you persuaded that young idiot to gamble,' he told her.

Without a word she opened her bag, threw down a bunch of notes on the table. The croupier changed them for her, and without counting the stack of chips she pushed them all onto eighteen. The ball whirled and bounced, came to rest in eighteen. The croupier pushed piles of chips across to her.

She said: 'Leave them.'

The wheel spun again; the ball rested in twenty. The chips on eighteen, representing over ten thousand pounds, were scooped up.

'Satisfied?' she sneered to Richard Glenning.

He smiled at her. He said: 'As a rule I dislike your type, but you rather interest me.'

'I'm grateful, kind sir. In what way do I interest you?'

'I don't know. You aren't very appealing to me physically, nor, I think, mentally.'

'Really? I apologise. I'm sorry I fall short of your aesthetic standards. How do I appeal to you?'

He considered. 'I think perhaps because I detest your kind so much. Spoilt and pampered society darlings, concerned only with themselves and their beauty and their lovers.'

'Perhaps you'd like to join the ranks of the lovers then?'

'It isn't that. Actually I'd like to give

you a damn good hiding, and take you down a peg or two.'

She was chuckling at some thought of her own. He said: 'What's the joke?'

'Don't you think I can see through you, idiot? Don't you think I can see you're playing a line to rouse my interest in you? You know the usual approach wouldn't work with me, don't you, so you try an entirely original angle. Well, it's original enough. You've got my interest. Now what?'

He smiled back at her, replied: 'You're pretty smart, aren't you? You know all the answers?'

'I ought to — providing the questions aren't too childish. What are you after, Mr . . . ?'

'I've told you my name — it's Glenning.'

'Oh, yes, Richard, isn't it? I'll call you Richard, then, since I find it easier to remember. What are you after, Richard?'

'What have you got?' he countered, still smiling.

'Plenty of time,' she told him. 'And a rather passionate nature if you'd care to cultivate it long enough.'

He said: 'Suppose we pay a visit to the bar? I talk so much better when I have a glass in my hand, don't you?'

She assented; she was interested in him, deeply. As he had thought, the unusual approach was essential to a girl of her type. She couldn't go for anything straight-forward, not the customary boy meets girl stuff, because everything, with her, and everything in her life, had to be a continual act. What the real woman beneath was like he had no idea; but the surface woman was all glitter and false colour.

For her part she was intrigued and attracted by him; and his statement that she didn't appeal to him physically or mentally, had determined her to find out if that were so, or if he had been, as she had said, just a 'line.'

When they had jostled a way to the bar, he said: 'What is a woman like you doing in a place like this?'

'Is there any place I'd fit in better?' she asked him, evasively, eyeing her drink. He offered her a smoke and lit one for himself. She glanced round at him, met his eyes and looked into them. She could not be sure what she read there; she had seen many things in the eyes of many men; passion, lust, love, hate and detestation. His were different altogether; there was interest, but she could not tell of what kind.

He said: 'Do you like this kind of thing?' and indicating the tables with a wave of his hands.

'It's better than dancing,' she told him. 'And not as enthrallin' as making love. I always come here when there's nothing better doing.'

'I see. I've noticed you rather a lot with the — the manager chap. Collwell, isn't his name? You seem quite attached to him.'

'You're rather nosey, aren't you, Richard? But if you're interested, I don't mind admitting that I have quite a 'soft spot' for Collwell, if you understand me. He's rather a nice type of man — there's nothing boorish about him . . . you take my meaning?'

'Meaning you find me boorish?' he chuckled.

'You are becoming a little too personal, aren't you? Suppose we discuss the weather?'

'Just as you like,' nodded Richard. 'It's been a warm day, hasn't it?'

'And it's quite likely to be a warmer night,' she told him, giving him a further glance from her veiled eyes. 'But hardly if we stay here. Wouldn't you care to take me out to dinner, Richard?'

He thought that one over; and decided in favour. He wanted to stick close to her, find out her reason for supporting Collwell's story. Could it be just that she was the man's mistress, or was there some deeper, and so far, hidden motive for it?

'If you insist,' he grinned, insolently. 'Where shall we go?'

'I know a pretty decent little place,' she told him. 'It's a Chinese restaurant, but they serve excellent English food.'

'I thought you'd have preferred the higher class establishments, Lady Mercia,' he said.

She smiled a bit drily.

'Did you? But they're so frightfully dull, aren't they? Definitely. Now at this place you never can tell what may happen. For instance, the time before last when I was there a man had — er — poison slipped into his soup! Don't you think that was rather novel?'

'I hope so,' he replied fervently, and wondered if there had been any special meaning behind her words. And then he got his first clue; he said: 'I'll wait here until you slip along to your room for your outdoor things.'

She raised her eyebrows. 'My dear Richard, what do you mean? My room? I can hardly slip along to the Ritz-Carlton you silly thing. Naturally my clothes are in the cloakroom here.'

'But I thought,' he said naturally, yet tensed in himself, 'you had a room here?'

'No; what made you think that?'

'Just that you seem to be always on the spot.'

She laughed. 'I have spent the night here once or twice. But I wouldn't take a room, believe me. I like something a little better. Wait here and I'll be back in a second.'

He waited, with plenty of food for

thought. So she wouldn't take a room there, eh? Yet, she claimed to have occupied the room Sheila had been sure had been hers. That was the first point he had received which corroborated Sheila's story, and he felt more determined than ever to go ahead to the bitter end now. Who knew what else he might learn?

Then she was back, and waited until he had picked up his coat and hat; they telephoned a cab, and she gave instructions to the driver.

The Chinese place she knew was in a side street off Soho. It wasn't a very exclusive place, and yet there were several of the upper strata dining there. The waiting was done by sleek, obsequious Chinamen in traditional tea gowns, with bland, smiling faces.

She ordered, and he sat back content to leave it to her. Her eyes were continually wandering round the room, stopping with interest at various people; and once or twice she nodded or smiled at various men. Seemingly she was quite well known here.

The food was good as she had said; but

the noise of the reed and string orchestra in the corner was abominable. He thought how well the atmosphere suited her strange personality. The lilt and whine of the Chinese rhythms, the swinging bead curtains, the smouldering incense holders before a carved figure of a Chinese dragon, and the very mystery and far away atmosphere of the entire place. For there was that same quality about her, and here her acting largely fell away, showing the sombre, serious eyed woman beneath the cloak.

He said, breaking the silence of ten minutes: 'You do like it here, don't you?'

She nodded, her eyes glowing with appreciation: 'I love it here. Why not? It's an escape from the life I know and lead. Here I can grasp a few minutes in quietness and silence and something of exoticism.'

'I'd hardly say quietness and silence,' he said, nodding at the jerky, manikin-like instrumentalists. She followed his gaze and laughed softly. She said: 'It does sound rather unpleasant at first, but it grows on you. The mystery of this place grows on you, doesn't it? Can't you sense it? Don't you think that waiter over there might quite easily be a pirate from a junk sailing down the Hoang-Ho? Or that one there a venerable old priest of some Confucian temple?'

'I hadn't thought you could be a romanticist,' he told her, looking at her with renewed interest. 'You seemed too cynical by far, too woman of the worldish for any sentimental stuff like you're giving me now. Is this another act like your sophisticated night clubbing society lady?'

'Who knows,' she shrugged. 'I'll leave you to figure that out for yourself. Perhaps the night clubbing sophisticate is the real me, and this is just an unreal phantasm of myself. Or this may be real, and the other Mercia false.'

'Or possibly they're both false, and now you're pulling a line to rouse my interest?' he challenged her.

'Possibly,' she admitted.

He decided to try a leading question. He said: 'I read a report about the death of a chap in the newspaper a few days ago. Man named Major Nesbitt, found in the Thames. I've an idea I saw him in the gambling rooms at the club not long ago. Did you know the chap by any chance?'

Her expression hadn't changed; her cigarette holder remained perfectly steady in her hand. She said: 'It's funny you should ask me a thing like that, isn't it? Ought I to have known him?'

'I thought you might, since you're often at the club.'

'I didn't. I hadn't even heard of him until you mentioned him this minute. Why *did* you mention him, Richard? Did you know him yourself?'

'No, I'm afraid not. I merely asked because I thought I may have spotted him around there, and I'm naturally interested in the poor chap. I wondered if you could supply a description of him, that was all.'

'I can't. I've never heard of him. I'm sorry if you're very disappointed.'

Her second slip! She claimed to have never heard of Nesbitt; yet she must have heard of him after the fuss Sheila had kicked up at the Club. Richard stowed that fact away in his mind and changed the topic.

'Personally I don't care much about him. Let's talk about you, shall we?'

'A fascinating subject. What do you want? My life history?'

'Something along those lines.'

She hesitated, then said: 'Well, I was born. I think that's the accepted procedure, although until I was five and a half I honestly believed I'd been found on a gooseberry bush. Then I grew up, and I didn't start going out alone with boys for ever so long. I led a very sheltered life, you know; in fact, I was every bit of eleven before I had my first date. With the butcher boy — ever such a charming fellow, but with a deplorable habit of dropping his sausages and aitches.

'Mind, mother was furious when she found out. But, of course, I outgrew him, and began to get around with quite a number of charming young gentlemen. They were all right but they were all rather over-eager. Young men always are. I rode a lot, and swam a lot, and went to Cowes and Goodwood and Epsom and all the best places. Then I made the acquaintance of Colly at a charity ball, and he quite attracted me. There was something dangerous about him. He brought me along to his club, and since then we've been rather good friends. Absolutely. Colly wants me to marry him — but of course I can't, and anyway he hasn't much money.'

'What? But he owns the club!'

'Oh, no. He only works for someone else. Someone he calls 'The Old Devil.' It's always 'the old devil wants me to do this,' or 'the old devil wants so and so doing'!'

5

'You Talk or Else . . . '

'That's interesting,' he said, casually, and since she didn't seem to have anything more to say about it, he allowed the matter to drop. The place was emptying now; the musicians — if they could be called that — had broken off for a bowl of some Chinese concoction, and peace reigned for the time being.

He had been so intent on what she had been saying that he had failed to notice the men who had entered. But his eyes now roved round the nearby tables, and he suddenly tensed.

There was no mistaking that these men were extremely interested in something at their table. There were about eight of them, all tough and hard-bitten, looking like the products of an American gangster film. They were hard-eyed and surly-faced; they were staring with fixed intensity at the table he and the girl occupied.

He looked at Mercia; now he could see it was this which had stopped her talking; she too was gazing at the men, and there was something of fear in her eyes.

'What is it?' he asked, lightly. 'You seem pretty interested in those plug uglies. Know them?'

She nodded. She said: 'I know them. They're a Soho gang — we must get out of here.'

'Get out? Why?' he echoed. 'Frightened of being kidnapped?'

She stirred impatiently. She said: 'I'm frightened — not of being kidnapped though.'

'But why should you be frightened of a Soho gang? You never did them any harm, did you?'

She didn't answer; she was pulling her fur cape about her, and collecting her gloves and handbag. She said: 'They may not be after me, but . . . ' It was almost muttered, hardly audible. But he heard it. She turned to him: 'Are you coming?'

'Naturally. Where do we go from here?'

'We may as well go to my rooms at the Ritz-Carlton if — if we can get there.'

'Any reason why we shouldn't?'

She got up suddenly. He rose with her. She walked first past the hard-faced men at the nearby tables, out to the exit. As she passed the last of them, a backward glance showed Richard that they had all eased round in their chairs and were following her with their eyes. But still they made no movement to get up.

Then they were outside, and she said: 'Hurry — please hurry!'

'But why not tell me what's going on? Are you in danger?'

'I may be. I'm not sure. That gang is very interested in the Satyr Club for some reason — I know they've brushed up against Colly before today. If they think I'm a friend of his . . . '

She broke off with a gasp of terror and said: 'Look!'

He half turned round to follow her glance behind — and saw the eight men streaming from the Chinese restaurant, moving softly and speedily after them. At the same time, from the shadows in front of them, emerged two more specimens.

He got the girl behind him, back to the wall; he set himself for trouble, and it wasn't long coming. The ten converged on him simultaneously, some of them carrying coshes, some carrying long wooden truncheons, with razor blades inserted in their split ends. They were, he saw, one of the gangs responsible for the great amount of razor slashing committed in the past few months. They were clever with their unusual weapons and for a moment he felt a twinge of panic. Then it passed, and he faced them grimly.

The leader was a beetle-browed gentleman in a tattered sports jacket and a muffler. His cloth cap was hauled down to the top of his bristling eyebrows, his battered ex-pugilistic nose was smeared across the better half of his features, his lips were open in a menacing snarl, showing rotted rows of teeth.

'All right, youse,' he snapped. 'Ain't going ter be no funny stuff round here if youse come along quiet.'

'And if we don't?' suggested Richard.

'You will, pal, you will. Or else . . . '

'What do you want with us?'

'Us? Why, we're kinda short of a coupla mugs to play a few games of ringsarosy, see? An' if we hadda lady we'd could also play the postman's knock, see? So you're comin' along, or else . . . '

Mercia said: 'Don't fight them — we'll have to go.'

But she might as well have spoken to a lump of stone. Richard said, quietly: 'All right, gentlemen. Come and get us.'

They did. At a sign from the beetle-browed gent they rushed forward, coshes and razors swinging. The leader was first in line, and he received the toe of Richard's shoe in his stomach, and retired promptly to the shadows to nurse his injuries. And then Richard had hastily snatched Mercia's bag from her hands, had held it by the long shoulder strap, and was laying about him with a fierce determination. It was a handy weapon, for the metalwork at the opening was strong and heavy. The thugs found themselves suffering nasty cuts and bruises, and there was a roar as one of them got the corner of the frame in his eye.

But it couldn't last that way for long, and the bag was suddenly seized and wrenched from Richard's fingers. They came in then, and one of the razor swingers drew a searing line down his arm, ripping his jacket and laying open his flesh. His fists found targets again and again, but at last he went down under a merciless hail of blows from the coshes.

Attention being concentrated on Richard for the moment, Mercia tried to dart away suddenly. The leader, just rising to his feet with a great pain still in his extensive abdomen, spotted her; his rock-like fist drove deep into her stomach, and retching violently she fell to the ground and lay panting to regain her breath.

'Awright fellers,' grunted the beetle-browed one. 'We c'n take 'em around by the side alleys. Kinda cluster round them then they won't be seen, see?'

The girl and her protector were hoisted, and with the gang all about them, concealing them from inquisitive eyes, they were carried away down narrow side streets, through into the heart of the slum section.

The thugs halted at an old warehouse, long since left derelict. Beetle-brow pushed open the old gates, and they surged through into the yard. Ahead was a dark building, musty smelling even from that distance, and towards this the captives were taken. The door again opened to the touch, admitting them into the building proper; across the concrete floor, past rotting sacks of grain, two of which beetle-brow pulled aside. Behind was revealed a short flight of steps running into the cellars. There was a connecting door which was closed, and beetle-brow knocked at this in a pre-arranged code.

A second's pause, and it opened.

The man who stood before them now was a strange contrast to the rest of the hooligans. He was tall and thin, with a small goatee beard, and a foreign appearance about him. His face was mournful-looking, as if he carried weighty sorrow on his thin shoulders. He stood aside and admitted the others, rubbed his emaciated hands as he observed the two captives.

'Ah! Excellent,' he chuckled. 'Excellent.'

Richard was still unconscious; they threw him to one side. Mercia, staring in fright about her, was fastened to some old pulley tackle which hung from the cellar ceiling, so that she was suspended helplessly in midair.

The thin man chuckled again, but there was something miserable even in his chuckle. He spoke in a high, whining voice: 'So glad you came to see me, my dear,' he told her, gloatingly. 'It's so very seldom we see a pretty face hereabouts, isn't it boys?'

The boys nodded.

'So very, *very* seldom. It really does get most boring at times, doesn't it boys?'

The boys said it did.

'And so you see, it's such a pleasure to have you with us,' he went on, almost bursting into tears. 'We do appreciate it, don't we boys?'

The boys said they did.

'We do love to have a pretty face — and — er — figure, here; with us, don't we boys?' went on the thin man.

The boys expressed wholehearted approval.

'What — what do you want with me?' stammered Mercia, all her charm and polished sophistication gone.

'Want? *Want*? Oh, of course. I will keep forgetting this is a business call,' said the thin man. 'Let me see, now . . . oh yes. You are the mistress of a man called Collwell, isn't that so?'

'No — no, I don't even know him. You must — must have got the wrong woman.'

He picked up her handbag which had been brought, snapped it open and rummaged amongst the contents. He brought out an engraved cigarette case, a couple of letters. He said: 'Funny you should be carrying Lady Standard's bag if you aren't Lady Standard. Don't continue to lie to us, please. We've seen you several times at the Chinese restaurant with Collwell. I wouldn't be surprised if he hadn't pointed us out to you.'

She saw it was hopeless to lie. She hung her head.

'You needn't worry, my dear,' he told her. 'We only require a little information. Perhaps you know that before Collwell was lucky enough to become manager of the Satyr Club, he led this gang? You do? Excellent, excellent. Perhaps you didn't know that when he left us, he left taking with him a little bag containing fifty thousand pounds, the takings of the gang for the past two years. Now we need that money very urgently . . . '

'Then why don't you get hold of Collwell?' she said, desperately.

'No, no, that would never do. I know Collwell, and with all his faults he's stubborn — you might call it brave. He'd stand any torture, any pain, rather than give in to us. We'd never find out where that little bag is. But you can — possibly you already know . . . '

'I don't — I swear I don't.'

'Hmm. Well, I'm a gentleman and I'll take your word. But you can find out, can't you?'

She was silent. He went on: 'Of course you can. You find that out for us, and if you can get the bag, get it. When we have that bag safely in our possession we can deal with Collwell as traitors should be dealt with. You understand?'

She nodded. He said: 'You agree?'

Again she nodded.

'Good. But remember this, Lady Standard — if you play us false — if you tell Collwell about this — if you don't find out what we wish to know . . . well, you have a fair idea of what the boys can do with their little weapons, haven't you? Suppose I get them to give you a demonstration now . . . ?' He made rapid signs to his thugs, and beetle-brow and another stepped forward.

He said: 'Cecil — that's the gentleman with the pushed in features, my dear, and don't let his name give you wrong ideas about him — Cecil is quite an expert with the razor. Show her, Cecil.'

The beetle-browed character suddenly swung, and the blade neatly severed the shoulder straps of her revealing gown, allowing the gown to slide down over her knees to the floor. Cecil licked his lips, began: 'Say, boss . . . '

'No!' snapped the thin man. 'Restrain your animal feelings, Cecil. Now then, you, Harry . . . '

Harry's specialty appeared to be the

cosh; he jumped in front of the girl, started lashing at her stomach; her entire body quivered and writhed under the assault, and thin shrieks tore from her throat. At last he stepped back, and the thin man himself pulled her gown into position, and tied the broken straps together.

'So you see, if you play us any tricks, you will be dead within a week. But before you die, I will turn the boys loose on you, and let you experience their pleasant little games. When you have the bag, or the secret of its whereabouts, you can find one of the boys any evening at the restaurant you so recently left. I will give you a full week — seven days from today, to secure it. If, at the end of that time, you have not succeeded, you will be found and brought here for more treatment. If you fail the second time, or if you inform Collwell that we are on the move, you *will* be killed! You understand all that?'

Sobbing painfully, she said: 'Yes . . . '

'Good. In fact, excellent.'

He turned to the unconscious Richard

on the floor, stirred him with his foot. He said: 'Hmm. Who is this?'

'He knows nothing about all this,' said the girl. 'He just happened to be with me. His name's Richard Glenning.'

'I see. In that case I don't think we need to injure him. He doesn't know where he's been, therefore he can't find us again. No, I think we can safely release this man . . . '

'Wait a minute, Pagan,' interrupted one of the others. 'How you know the skirt won't split on our hidey hole?'

'What good would it do her?' enquired Pagan. 'We aren't here often — and if she did split we'd know, and she'd suffer accordingly. She knows that, don't you, my dear?'

'Yes,' nodded Mercia.

'Excellent. Go through this man's pockets and take what you find, boys. Then you can take them both back to where you made the attack on them. Lay him in the street, and knock out the girl as well. And you, my dear, when he regains his wits, tell him you have been set on by a bunch of thieves, and robbed.

Be sure and say nothing about this place, or else . . . '

'I — I understand.'

'In that way he won't even know he's been here — oh, dear, you'd better administer another dose, Harry. He appears to be coining round.'

Richard was groaning and stirring. Harry bent low, whammed his cosh against the senseless man's head again.

'Now you can release the woman.'

Mercia was cut down, and collapsed in a heap on the floor, bent double with the agony in her stomach. Pagan said: 'Poor dear. She seems to be suffering rather badly. Harry, suppose you attend to her? Give her a shot of morphia to take away the pain?'

Grinning, Harry stepped up behind the girl, leaned over and brought the cosh thudding down. Pagan smiled at the two bodies, looked at his thugs sadly. He said: 'Take them right back, boys, won't you?'

The boys said they would.

'I wouldn't like *anything* to happen to the lady on the way, Cecil . . . ' he added meaningfully.

'Awright, boss. I'll behave meself.'

'Yes; well, off you go, boys. It's been a very pleasant evening, and I consider we should have the money back before long. The girl is a coward; she knows we mean what we threaten, and I think she'll keep her part of the bargain. But in any event we won't risk using this place again. In future we'll find a fresh headquarters. Meet me at Louie's when you've done that little job, and well talk it over.'

And he remained smiling at the cellar door long after the boys had transported their inanimate burdens out of the place.

A peculiar smile. At length, he said to himself: 'Really, the boys are most thoughtless. I wonder if they have any idea what I mean to do when I get that money . . . Fifty thousand! Just enough to set me up in luxury for the rest of my life!'

He was almost laughing outright now, and still his face looked as miserable as sin. It was a trick of his features which were so formed as to give a perpetual droop to his lips. But inside he felt quite elated. Fifty thousand pounds — all for himself!

Of course, he would have to attend to the boys, too; he didn't want them trying to exact reprisals . . . a burning building would take care of them — very nicely . . .

6

Re-Enter Sheila

Richard came to, his head feeling as if it would split at any minute. He pressed his hands to it and groaned, then pulled himself into a sitting position.

They were still in the narrow street where they had been attacked. It was still dark, but he could feel the girl's body near him, almost pressed against him. He fumbled for his lighter, found it, flicked it on.

Mercia was in a bad way; the cosh had split the skin of her temple, and a trickle of blood was running down onto her face. Added to that her fur cape had fallen aside, revealing two long, red cuts, very thin and fine, but bleeding quite profusely. This, had he known it, was where Cecil's razor had slashed her when cutting her shoulder straps.

The straps themselves, still knotted,

had slipped from her smooth skin, and now the gown had fallen from her body as far as the thighs. Her underthings were ripped above the stomach, as if by blows from some heavy weapon, and beneath could be seen purple, swollen patches of skin, and blueish coloured bruises.

He gave an exclamation of anger, raised her head to his knee, and fished in his rear pocket for the flask of whisky he always carried.

The liquid revived her almost at once; and in another minute she was adjusting her gown on her shoulders again, and pushing back her hair which was somewhat bedraggled.

'The police,' Richard said. 'We'll have to get hold of them as soon as possible — maybe it isn't too late for them to nab that bunch of cut-throats.'

She shook her head, laid a restraining hand on his arm.

'No, Richard, please. I — I don't want the police to know about this — do this for me, please. Don't mention it to anyone.'

'But Mercia — Good God, look what

they've done to you! You can't mean you'd let them get away with that, surely?'

She coloured. She said: 'Richard, believe me, if the police are told something worse would happen to me. I know it. Please do as I ask and don't mention it to a soul. Will you?'

'I don't understand . . . what did happen? How did you come to be beaten — in such a place, and to get those gashes on your shoulders?'

'I — I don't know, Richard. I must have been unconscious when they did it.'

'But what was their motive?'

'I — I think it was only robbery,' she lied lamely.

'I can't believe that. That beetle-browed specimen spoke as if we were to be taken somewhere. And you yourself didn't seem to think they were after us for robbery — remember you said . . . '

'I know what I said. But — well, we weren't taken anywhere, were we? And my money is missing, so it must have been robbery. But I do know the gang — I do know they'd kill me — you as well — if they thought we'd been to the police.'

'I think we were taken somewhere,' he said keenly. 'Otherwise how did this dust get on my jacket?'

He indicated several smears of dry dust, such as settles in old, disused buildings, to her. She bit her lip, said: 'Richard, I'm sorry you had to go through all this, I really am. But please do as I ask and give the police a miss. For my sake.'

He grunted, but said: 'Very well. Do you feel able to walk?'

She nodded, and he helped her to her feet. She started to limp along, with his arm supporting her. Once or twice she stumbled, for her head ached terribly, and the punishment she had taken had made her feel weak in the legs. At the first major road they picked up a taxi, and he gave an address. She said: 'Where are you taking me?'

'To my flat, of course. You can't go anywhere else until you've been fixed up — your gown is stained with blood, and your face is a frightful mess from the blood from your temple. No one will see you if we use the servants' entrance.'

She silently acquiesced. Had she gone

back to the Satyr Club, Collwell might have seen her, and wanted to know just where she had been, what she had been up to. She daren't tell him. She knew quite well the thugs hadn't been playing with her, and that unless they knew where that bag with the money it contained was hidden, they would get her and kill her no matter how far she ran. She had a wholesome respect for the Soho boys and their miserable-looking chief.

They reached his apartments without being seen; and he gave her a dressing gown of his and some pajamas to wear; she changed in the bedroom, and used the strips of sticking plaster he had found for her liberally. When she came out with her gown he had made strong coffee, and he took the blood stained gown from her.

'There's a sixty-minute cleaner's round the corner,' he told her. 'I'll have this sent along.'

'But — what will they think?'

'It doesn't matter. They aren't paid to think.'

She sipped coffee while he was gone; he came back in a few minutes and took a seat beside her on the settee. She didn't say anything, because she couldn't think of anything to say. She knew his eyes were on her, speculatively, and she knew he wasn't at all satisfied with the story she had told him. He said: 'What happened while I was unconscious?'

'I've told you — I don't know, honestly. Don't you believe that?'

'Hardly. This dust on my jacket is plain enough indication that we were taken somewhere. Nor do I believe that they did that to your stomach while you yourself were out. There wouldn't have been any sense in it. Why not be frank with me? Were they trying to make you talk?'

For a second she felt a ridiculous desire to tell him about it all, to nestle her head into him and seek his sympathy and help. But she curbed the instinct. She couldn't put him in possession of the true facts, there was no telling what he might take it into his head to do. He went on: 'You know we were taken somewhere, don't you?'

She shook her head stubbornly: 'How should I? I was knocked out as well as you, wasn't I? If we were taken somewhere I know nothing about it.'

He scowled angrily into the electric fire which he had switched on. She moved her leg slightly so that the dressing gown fell off just above the knee, revealing her round, rosy limbs. He ignored this old gag, suddenly barked: 'You don't want me to go to the police, do you?'

'No — Richard, you mustn't.'

'Then I'll give you one more chance to tell me. If you insist you don't know I'll ring the police up and have them down here.'

'You couldn't! You wouldn't do anything like that. It would be in all the newspapers — my aunt would — would be furious if she knew I patronised low cafés in Soho. She'd — she'd cut me off without a penny.'

'What has your aunt to do with it?' he demanded.

'She's awfully rich — and awfully mean. And very, very moral. You know the kind. I haven't much money of my own, and she's getting on in years, and I'm relying on her legacy . . . you see. If she read of anything like this . . . '

'That isn't the real reason, is it?'

'It's one of them.'

'But it's a lie, for my benefit. If you're so hard up as you make out, how did you manage to gamble a thousand pounds tonight, and not pick the winnings up when you won?'

'That wasn't a loss for me. The Satyr Club sort of employ me to get the games going. They give me so much money every night and I use it at the tables. It encourages others who happen to be a bit nervous, when they see Lady Standard gambling there. So I could easily afford to lose that, you see.'

It sounded quite plausible, and he believed that part of it. It had seemed to him at the time that there was something phoney about the cool way she had gambled that money. But still he didn't like to confess himself satisfied. He said: 'I'm quite confident your aunt wasn't the only reason, even now. I'm still determined to go ahead with my call to the police — after all, I myself have been robbed of a little over five hundred, you know. How about that? And I don't get money given to me to throw away.'

'Don't make that call, Richard. I can't tell you any more. But you won't make it . . . you like me too much already!' She was sidling nearer to him, so that the firmness of her leg was against his, now; he could feel her warm, scented breath fanning against his neck as he bent towards the fire; and her soft fingers played with his hair and stroked the nape of his neck; she leaned closer still, until her supple figure was pressing on his shoulder, until, in spite of himself, he felt desire rising within him.

'Don't think about it anymore,' she pleaded, 'and then you and I can be such good — friends. But if you 'phone for the police, Richard, I won't speak to you ever again. Promise?'

He stood up abruptly; he snapped: 'But damn it all, Mercia, it isn't fair . . . thugs like those shouldn't be allowed to wander round at large. The police will have them in no time if we give descriptions . . . '

'They won't, Richard. You don't know Pagan and his . . . oh!'

He started: 'So that's the name of one of them, is it?' he grunted. 'You know a lot more than you like to say, don't you?'

She caught his hand and drew him down beside her. The touch of her fingers electrified him, and the nearness of her perfume scented hair intoxicated him. Her lips were red, and moist, and full of invitation. He cursed: 'You're a damnable little witch, Mercia. I hate your kind, but . . .'

She smiled up at him, and the next moment his lips were hard against her own, his arms were about her waist and hers about his neck.

They clung together, locked in that embrace for minutes; and even then they would not have parted but for the voice which spoke from the doorway . . .

'Oh! I'm sorry, Mr. Glenning. I didn't know you had *company*!'

It snapped the spell she had woven over him, and he drew away.

Sheila — for it was she who had entered — was turning to leave, and he said: 'Don't go, Sheila. Please come in.'

She came in, her eyes resting somewhat

scornfully on the pair. He said: 'This — er — this is — hem — Lady Standard — Sheila Nesbitt.'

'We've met, I think,' drawled Mercia, slipping at once into her habitual pose.

'We have,' agreed Sheila, icily.

'Definitely. You're the little girl who made such a show of herself at the Satyr Club, aren't you, my dear?'

'And you're the little girl who made such a liar of herself at the same place,' flared back Sheila. 'You seem to have rather a taste for being partly dressed, Lady Standard.'

'Hmm! I can see it's going to be an intensely jolly evening, absolutely,' drawled Mercia, patting her hair into place and drawing the gown over her legs. 'I had no idea you two knew each other this well . . .'

The glance she darted at Richard was keen and suspicious. He mumbled something totally inadequate, and silently cursed his luck.

Sheila said: 'I'm so sorry I burst in on such a touching little scene — I did knock, but didn't get any answer. I suppose it was because you were so — busy?'

'Well, you see,' began Richard, and broke off as there was a loud rap at the outer door. Sheila opened it, came back with a parcel, said: 'The page just handed this in. It seems to have Lady Standard's name on it.'

'Ah, yes,' sighed Mercia. 'My dress. Well, I'll climb into it and move on, I think. The company here's a bit vulgar for my liking, I'm afraid.'

'It is rather vulgar,' agreed Sheila. 'But I think there'll be a considerable improvement when you've left.'

Mercia smiled, went into the bedroom with her dress. Sheila said nothing while she waited, and Richard didn't want to say anything until they had seen the last of Mercia. Eventually she came out, walked over to Richard, kissed him lightly, and said:

'It's pretty evident to me that you're going to be busy for the rest of the night, Dicky . . . so I'll pop along old thing. You might give me a ring tomorrow — if not, I'll give you one. Good night.'

She went, with Sheila glaring after her. There was a silence in the room, then

Sheila said: 'I'd better say what I have to say and go. I expect my reputation's at stake every minute I spend here.'

'No, no, you're wrong,' cut in Richard quickly. 'Honestly. I was just trying to get some information out of her. That's all. You don't think a woman like her could appeal to me, do you?'

'But — but her dress?'

He explained rapidly, omitting nothing, not even the way he had succumbed to her allure. Sheila seemed to understand when he had finished his story, and she said, contritely:

'Oh, dear. You were doing so well, and now she'll know you're up to something. I'm so sorry . . . but . . . '

'Don't worry about it. You couldn't have helped it, since you couldn't have known I'd got quite so far in such a short time.'

'But I could — I could have sneaked out again . . . '

'Yes, you might have done that,' he admitted, ruefully.

'But, you see . . . ' She broke off awkwardly.

'But what?'

She flushed, stammered: 'I — I was wild . . . '

'You were? About what?'

'I — I thought you were letting that woman make a fool of you — I — of course, it doesn't really matter what I think I suppose . . . '

'But it does,' he said softly, placing his hands on her shoulders. 'Are you trying to say you were jealous?'

'I expect that's what it was — in a way . . . '

He drew her towards him; she said: 'Dick — don't!'

'Why not?'

'I don't know; for one thing though, I've only known you this week . . . and you've just been kissing that other — woman!'

'That was business,' he told her seriously. 'This is pleasure.'

And he kissed her determinedly, first on the point of her nose, then on her lips. She seemed to enjoy it, but pushed him away after a second. She sat down, and he said: 'Are you back here for good now?'

She nodded; she said: 'Or at least until I find out the people who had a hand in father's death. I — I buried mother days ago . . . '

'I'm awfully sorry, Sheila. How do you feel about it now? Pretty cut up I expect?'

'Not — not so bad, now, thanks,' she said, trying to smile. 'It was a bit of a shock to me though when I came in and found you with Lady Standard. You know, Dick, you're the only friend I have now.'

'I know; and believe me I'll help all I can. I've already found out a little. And I'll carry on with my rooms at the Satyr Club until I find out some more.'

'But do you think it's safe after having been seen with me? She's in on the plot — she'll tell Collwell.'

He said, thoughtfully: 'I don't think she will tell Collwell too hastily. Wait a minute, and we'll see . . . '

He thumbed the telephone directory, found a number. He dialed, listened. He said: 'Lady Standard? Good! This is Richard Glenning. I'd advise you not to mention the fact of my knowing Miss Nesbitt to anyone, Lady Standard — or

possibly I may have a few things to tell
the local constabulary about tonight!
Good night!'

7

Lady Standard's Aunt

Richard returned to his room at the Satyr later that night, leaving Sheila in possession of the flat. She was worried for him now that Lady Standard knew he was connected with her, but he was quite certain Lady Standard wouldn't betray him in view of the fact that he could also make things slightly unpleasant for her.

As on the previous nights, however, he found out precisely nothing. And as he was leaving the Club the following morning, he bumped into Mercia, just about to enter.

'My dear man,' she said lightly, with no reference to his last night's 'phone call. 'How nice to see you again. You're in a position to do me rather a favour; absolutely.'

'Favour?' he questioned. 'Another?'

'Yes. I always seem to be asking favours of you, don't I?'

'Something else you don't want me to mention?' he asked.

'Oh, no, not this time, dear thing. I simply thought you could help me to pass a boring afternoon — could you? Or have you — er — another engagement?'

He confessed he hadn't. Nothing important. She rippled: 'That's delightful. You see, every month I pay a duty visit to my old aunt, you know. Kind of keeping an eye on my legacy, if you see what I mean.'

'I think I do.'

'Yes; well, today's the day as it were. She's fabulously rich but frightfully mean; definitely so. Lives just outside of the city, with an old maid like herself. I really must go, but I positively loathe the idea of facing boiled eggs and crumpets all by myself at five in the afternoon. That's why I'd like you to come along, Dicky dear. You will?'

'Why not your friend Colly?' he suggested.

She pooh-poohed the notion. 'I could hardly take Colly. The poor man does his best, but it absolutely sticks out a mile that he's no gentleman. And she's so dashed fond of gentlemen, you see. That's how I came to think of you — aren't you flattered?'

'At present — but I expect I'll be flat-*tened* before the afternoon's over. However, if it means so much to you I'll come.'

'Yes, do. You'll simply loathe Aunt Abigail, but for my sake, make yourself pleasant, won't you? She has her interesting side, you know. The old dear's quite a character at times.'

'Hmm. What time shall I see you?'

'I think two o'clock. I'll call round for you in my car, if you like.'

He left her with those arrangements, and the entire way back to his flat he was wondering just what she was getting up to now.

He told Sheila about the arrangement, and she tried to puzzle it out also. It seemed too unreal to be straightforward; but what benefit Mercia might derive by inducing Richard to spend a boring afternoon with her rich aunt, she couldn't think. At last she said: 'I think she's doing it to make me jealous, Dick. I'm sure she is.'

'But that's ridiculous. She doesn't think anything of me so why should she?'

Sheila shook her head: 'She does think quite a lot of you. I could tell that last night when I walked in. You may think not, but women can generally tell about these things.'

He laughed at that theory and kissed her. 'I'll go along, anyway. I may still find out something from her. You never can tell.'

And he did go along. At two, a long, sleek sports car rolled up to the front of the building and Lady Standard tootled merrily at the horn. He came down, and climbed in, and Sheila watched him going from the window, not missing the sneering glance Mercia threw at her as the car drove away.

It was a pleasant run, and Mercia talked inanely most of the time; so much so that he said: 'Look here, Mercia, can't you be yourself for a bit?'

'Myself?'

'Yes, yourself. Stop putting on that act

of yours. Last night when we ran into trouble, you were different entirely. Now you've drifted back to the 'absolutely,' and 'definitely' and 'old thing' routine.'

'But my dear old thing, that is myself.'

'Then I don't like it; it irritates me.'

'All right, Richard, just as you say. I'll be the sweet, innocent young virgin for you if you wish.'

He grunted and they drove on in silence until they reached a medium-sized, yellow-stone mansion on the outskirts of the city.

Even from the drive it looked old fashioned and dusty; as if it belonged in another age; and from the demurely curtained windows a face peered out . . .

'That's the old fleabag herself,' exclaimed Lady Standard. 'Ugh! That's all she ever does — sits and watches who's coming and who's going, you know. Too bad, isn't it? But I suppose it's all you can do when you're seventy-seven. She's got an ambition to live to be a hundred — God alone knows why! We'll have a lovely time listening to her talking about her ailments all day. Ten to one she talks about her ulcers while we're eating the boiled eggs!'

The car had stopped, the front door opened, and an old maid came doddering down the steps.

'The maid-companion,' whispered Mercia. 'Been with auntie for fifty years, God help her. I have to kiss her, but you needn't bother.'

They left the car, and the maid-companion quavered a greeting; Mercia dutifully pecked her on the cheek, and she simpered coyly at Richard. 'Is this your young man, dear?'

'Sort of,' admitted Mercia.

'Oh, my! Your auntie will be pleased to see him. She's often said to me you should be thinking of getting married. Come on in, dear, and your young man too. Come on in.'

And she hobbled up the steps into the interior of the place which smelt of dust and dry woodwork.

'Isn't it positively nauseating?' whispered Mercia.

Richard said: 'I don't think so. It's just that it doesn't fit in with your kind of life, does it?'

'Does it with yours?' she asked, giving

him an impudent look.

He admitted it didn't, quite.

They were shown into a sitting-room, littered with bric-à-brac, old brass, old silver, and old aunts. She was still sitting by the window, squinting through pince-nez at some knitting she held, and attired in dingy black and a violently coloured shawl.

Her face was lined, her hair silver, and her movements feeble; yet there was something strong in the features them-selves. Her body was shapeless, like most old things. She croaked:

'How nice to see you again my dear. Do sit down . . . '

Mercia dutifully kissed her, and intro-duced Richard. She said: 'This is a gentleman friend of mine, auntie Abigail. I thought it would be a nice afternoon for him to come and see you with me.'

The old aunt surveyed him keenly over the tops of her glasses; then she said: 'How do you do, young man. Sit down, won't you? Are you the young man Mercia intends to marry?'

'Er — well — I — '

'Don't embarrass poor Richard, auntie,' said Mercia. 'We haven't decided yet.'

'Hmm. Richard's his name, is it?'

'Richard Glenning,' elucidated Mercia.

There was a momentary lull, then, with a resigned look at Dick, Mercia said: 'How's your lumbago, auntie?'

The old woman put on a suffering expression. 'It's awful,' she admitted, sounding like an early Christian martyr. Shocking. Doctor Fust visits me every day now — think of the bills, my dear! I don't know how I'll ever manage to pay them.'

'I'm sorry to hear that,' said Mercia. 'You must take good care of yourself . . . '

'Oh, I will, I will, don't worry. But Esmerelda — that's my maid, young man — ' she added, to Richard, 'upsets me at times. She will insist on buying the dearest household coal, and I really can't afford it, you see. I'm only a poor old woman. It's awful. Do you know, we had the window cleaner this year, and he actually charged three shillings for a mere twenty windows! He wanted five, but I soon put a stop to *that* kind of profiteering.'

Mercia raised her eyes to the ceiling,

then continued, courageously.

'And your hearing?'

'Oh, my dear, that's shocking. Really shocking. I can hardly hear you talking, my child. I have to strain to catch every word ... Doctor Fust says there isn't anything the matter with my ears, but he doesn't know, he doesn't know anything at all. I don't know why I keep him on, what with those terrible bills he charges.'

'My God, isn't this awful,' muttered Mercia out of the side of her mouth, to Richard. The old woman suddenly said: 'What's awful?'

'Er — oh, nothing, dear. I simply said it isn't lawful the price they charge for treatment nowadays,' said Mercia hastily.

'Humph! Thought you said something was awful. You haven't much to say for yourself young man, have you?' she directed at Dick.

'Hasn't been much chance so far,' he replied politely, and the old woman chuckled to herself.

'No,' she said, 'and there won't be. When you get as old as I am, young fellow, you like to talk as much as you can, because you haven't long left to talk in, you see.'

'Oh, I wouldn't say that,' began Mercia.

'What *would* you say then?' snapped Aunt Abigail. 'And what do you know about it anyway? You're only a child.'

She knitted a little while Mercia cooled off. Richard couldn't help grinning a little. The old lady tickled him, and it was amusing to see how easily she handled the expectant heiress.

After a time, Aunt Abigail called: 'Esmerelda . . . *Tea*! She'll get our teas now' she told them. 'But she's so slow, I always have to tell her an hour before-hand . . . what would you like, young, fellow?'

'I really can't say I'm particular . . . '

'Well, you'll have a boiled egg, then; Mercia loves boiled eggs, don't you, child?'

'Adore them,' grunted Mercia.

'They're rather expensive — I have to pay twopence each for them . . . but I like people who come to see me to have something nice to eat.'

'Oh my God,' muttered Mercia.

'What was that?' grunted Aunt Abigail.

'Oh — I said you're very good, auntie dear,' supplied Mercia.

'I should think I am — eggs for tea at twopence a time!'

Tea came up, served in leisurely fashion by Esmerelda, who then joined the party for her own tea. The tea was weak and insipid, the eggs watery and half cooked, and the scones, which Esmerelda had made with her own gnarled hands, doughy. Mercia gagged on the last of her egg and put down her spoon. Aunt Abigail rapped: 'Eat that egg up, Mercia. I don't like people to waste good food!'

Dutifully, but with a long face, Mercia ate it up. Afterwards, at Mercia's suggestion, she and Dick went out to see the garden, and from somewhere Mercia produced a camera.

'How about passing time by taking a few photographs, Dick?' she asked him, and he nodded. He took one of her standing by the sweet peas, and one of her reclining on the grass. Then she took one of him.

'The sun's facing the house,' she told

him. 'Suppose we take it with you standing against the wall there? Should come up nicely.'

'Here?' he asked, taking a position.

'More to the right, Dick — a little bit back — that's it. Stay there — *now!*'

It was a small portion of stone falling past his eyes which gave him the warning. He acted quickly; even as he had glanced up and seen a massive portion of the stone parapet which was cracked and broken tottering over the edge, he threw himself sideways full length. The stone-work, which must have weighed almost five hundredweights, toppled down and smashed into the soft soil. He picked himself up, shuddered as he saw how far it had dug in, and wondered what he would have been like had he been beneath it!

Mercia was staring towards him with wide open eyes; but he thought he detected something of disappointment in her glance.

Good Heavens,' she said. 'You might have been — killed!'

'Yes,' he retorted. 'Wouldn't that have

108

been fortunate for certain people?'

She ignored the pointed remark, said: 'I've noticed that loose piece many times. I've meant to warn auntie to have it fixed, but I always forgot. Thank God nothing happened.'

He said: 'Rather unusual that it should suddenly decide to fall just after you'd worked me into a suitable position for receiving it, wasn't it?' He stared up at the roof.

'Dick! What are you saying . . . ?'

'You know damned well,' he rapped, whirling on her. 'This was all arranged, wasn't it?'

'Dick!'

'Oh, don't give me that innocent stuff,' he snapped. 'You had someone up on the roof to push that stone over. It would have been an unfortunate accident, wouldn't it? Very clever of you to try to stage it down here, where no one could have suspected foul play. Your old aunt would have made a good blind for you, wouldn't she? She could have testified it was an accident — you wouldn't have stood in any danger of being accused of having a hand in it!'

'Honestly, Dick ... I didn't have anything to do with it.'

'You can save that — I know you did. I'm going to take a look on the roof, if you don't mind.'

He moved quickly round to the back of the house; there was an old fire escape installed there, running right to the flat roof. But he didn't mount it; for over the field behind the house, well away by now, was the figure of a running man. And there was something familiar about the set of his back!

Richard looked hard; he thought he recognised that back; and when the man momentarily turned, he felt sure the features were those of Collwell, manager of the Satyr Club!

Collwell! That explained everything, of course. Mercia had told Collwell of his connection with Sheila Nesbitt; Collwell had enlisted her aid to have him put out of the way. Whose idea it had been he could not be certain, but he thought it was probably Mercia's.

Mercia had said she knew about that

loose stone; probably she had arranged to bring Dick down here, get him into position, for Collwell to drop that stone on! But for the piece of loose stuff which had fallen first, he would have been squashed flat, and almost certainly killed, under that heavy masonry.

He walked back thoughtfully to the front garden; Mercia was no longer there, and he went into the house, found her in the sitting-room with her aunt. The aunt looked at him as he came in, and said: 'I believe you had a nasty accident, young man?'

'I did,' he admitted, not caring to say he thought it had been more than a simple accident. 'Fortunately I'm still able to stand up.'

'I'm so sorry — about the accident I mean,' said the old woman. 'It's really my fault for not having that stone fixed. But masons and bricklayers want such a lot of money these days, don't they? I was waiting to see if I could persuade some local lad to do it for a few shillings, you see. The milkman said he would. I never thought . . . '

'It doesn't matter,' Dick told her. 'No harm done. Well, isn't it time we were pushing back to town, Lady Mercia?'

They took their leave of the old ladies, and she followed him silently to her car . . .

8

Collwell Checks Out

'So you see.' said Dick, to Sheila, later that same night. 'You were dead wrong about Mercia thinking anything of me. And her motive was a bit deeper than merely jealousy, after all.' He gave a sudden chuckle.

Sheila said: 'What are you laughing at? It isn't at all funny. I warned you not to go.'

'I was laughing at something I said to Mercia when she first asked me to go,' he replied. 'She said I ought to be flattered to be asked — and I replied I'd probably be flat-*tened* before the afternoon was out. It must have given her a good laugh to know just how right I was, unintentionally.'

'Many a true word spoken in jest,' clichéd Sheila. 'But it is the limit. Of course you can't prove anything, can you?'

'Afraid not. But I'm going to have a

113

little heart to heart talk with Collwell shortly. I'll slip along to the club now, I think.'

Meanwhile, at the Satyr Club, gaming was in full swing; Collwell was standing rubbing his hands by the end table, watching the money roll in. Tonight was the night, he was thinking; fifty thousand he had stolen from the members of his former gang — and over a hundred thousand from the gaming rooms themselves. With tonight's takings it was his intention to skip out and take a boat to parts unknown.

'The old devil' would be furious. But he didn't see that much could be done about him if they had no idea where he'd got to. He had to get out of it; that Richard Glenning, Mercia had told him about was snooping too much; he had an idea that the club and its gaming tables were going to be unhealthy before very long. And he hated anything that was unhealthy.

He chuckled again as the suckers poured their chips onto the tables, and the croupier spun the wheel. More and more rolled into the bank; it was the best night the bank had had for a long time, even though the tables were crooked.

He decided to go and pack his bag; he wanted to skip right after the place closed, and he had already scheduled the boat he would take. It left at two a.m.; there would be just time to catch it.

He turned and walked through the green baize door which connected the gaming rooms with the hotel part of the premises. He used the electric lift to reach his own luxurious suite of rooms, which were on the top floor.

He started slightly as he noticed the door of the room he used as a study was slightly ajar — and hurried forward when he took in the fact that the light was switched on!

'Come right in, Colly,' murmured Lady Mercia, who was seated on one corner of the desk, swinging her silk stockinged legs.

'Mercia . . . what . . . what the devil . . . ?'

He stared foolishly at the neat little automatic she held, shivered as he noted it was fitted with a silencer. Then his eyes gradually wandered to the desk; and the safe behind, the door of which swung idly open! On the desk itself was a black bag — a black bag which he knew only too well.

'Mercia . . . '

'Sit down!'

Her hard tone of voice warned him she was not to be trifled with. He was going to have a good deal of explaining to do.

She said: 'It was an unlucky day for you when I contacted you and engaged you to run this place, wasn't it? Very unlucky. Of course, you'd have been all right, Colly, if you'd not tried to chisel us! But we don't stand for chiselers . . . '

'Mercia, you're wrong. Listen . . . that money in the bag belongs to me and no one else. It's what I made from the other gang I used to run.'

'You walked out on them with a hundred and fifty thousand pounds?'

'That's it. That's the truth. I got it from the proceeds of the other mob of boys.'

'You're a liar,' she snarled, and her eyes were cold and merciless above the muzzle of the gun. 'You ran out on them with *fifty thousand* — the other hundred you got from this club!'

'I didn't . . . '

'Oh, but you did, Colly. You didn't know I'd had a word with Pagan, did you?'

'False-face Pagan?' gasped Collwell.

'That very same. And he told me you ran out with fifty thousand. He seemed very anxious to regain it, dear man. I'm afraid he'll be rather unlucky, but still . . . I had meant to take it back, but on thinking it over I rather imagine I'll take my chances. That's beside the point, however . . . it's mainly this *extra* hundred thousand I'm annoyed about, Colly.'

'I was keeping it here — for the club,' he stammered. 'I meant to hand it over to you eventually.'

'That's intriguin'. But if it's true, why had you booked a berth on a liner, leaving tonight? Oh, yes, I found the ticket in the safe with the money. Explain that away, Colly, old thing — if you can!'

He couldn't, and he didn't try. He said:

'What's your next move?'

She swung her legs, idly. She said: 'I'm going to pull this trigger, old thing. It'll go 'pop!' and then you'll be just another body for James to get rid of. Easy, isn't it?'

'You daren't — the old devil will . . . '

'I've been in touch with the old devil,' smiled Mercia. 'I've had orders to carry out your execution.'

He tried one last angle. He pleaded: 'Mercia — after all we've been to each other, you couldn't kill me like this.'

'Been to each other? Really, Colly, you rather flatter yourself. I admit you were entertainin' for a night or two — but one outgrows men so quickly. Besides, you muffed that job on Richard Glenning this afternoon, and you really deserve punishing for that. But it doesn't matter now . . . Glenning can be attended to later, and that girlfriend of his. At the moment it's you I'm seein' to.'

He knew by her face it was useless to argue; he wasn't kidding himself about Mercia — her name was a mockery, the exact opposite of the woman herself.

There was no mercy at all in her entire body. She said, softly: 'Get up and close the door!'

'Why should I?'

He had nerve; he wasn't any coward, as False-face Pagan had said. She smiled again, said: 'Because I'm not very particular where you get it. I may give it you in the temple where it won't make quite so much mess. Or I may give it you in the stomach. But I'll be inclined to be easier with you if you get up and shut the door like a gentleman.'

He nodded; he got up, quite calmly. He walked across and threw the door shut. He came back and sat down.

'I do so hope you aren't going to make a lot of noise about it,' she complained. 'I hate to hear men squealing like stuck pigs, and supposing I miss a vulnerable spot first time, you're liable to kick up such a fuss.'

'Don't worry,' he told her. 'I won't squawk. Mind if I smoke first?'

'Well, you can light up. But I haven't much time to spare, so I'm afraid I can't let you finish it. I'm sorry.'

He nodded and lit up, inhaling deeply. He said: 'Go ahead!'

His fingers, holding the cigarette, were as steady as rocks. She raised the gun; she said: 'I hate to do this, really, Colly. You really have got a nerve, and I admire that. But unfortunately, I have my instructions. And anyway, you are rather a rat.'

He said: 'I'm waiting.'

She pulled gently on the trigger; her aim didn't slide off target. A neat round hole shattered its way into Collwell's forehead.

He didn't fall; he sat there on the chair, cigarette still held smouldering between his fingers. But his eyes were the eyes of a dead man!

She sighed and murmured to herself: 'Poor Colly. Such a graceful way of passing out, too. He really does look such a lamb sitting there, with that cigarette he isn't able to use any more. Oh, dear, it's a hard life.'

She slid from the desk, slipped the gun into her bag; she pulled the wrinkles out of her stockings, straightened the seams. Then she collected the black bag from the desk. She crossed the office to leave, opened the door — and stared at Richard Glenning!

'Well,' he said brightly, 'quite a pleasant little surprise, isn't it? How are you feeling after your exertions of this afternoon, my dear Lady Standard?'

She blocked the doorway, drawled: 'Just fine. How are you?'

'Great, great. I came along to have a word with friend Collwell who shoved that nasty big chunk of stone onto me — or tried to. James told me he was up here — is he?'

'He is; but he isn't seeing anyone.'

'He'll see me.'

'I assure you he won't see anyone. That's the truth. So you might just as well be getting along, Richard.'

'Nonsense. Colly's pleased to see me at any time. Ah, there he is — rather rude of him to keep his back turned, isn't it?'

He peered more closely past her shoulder. He said: 'Hello! Is he asleep?'

'Yes, he is. He's sound asleep. Worn out in fact. He'd be annoyed if you disturbed him. Now push along and don't make such a perfect pest of yourself, old thing. Let the man grab his forty winks.'

Richard sniffed — hard. 'Smell of cordite or something like that around here, isn't there?' he said, with sudden suspicion.

'Is there? I don't smell it.'

'I don't expect you would with all that perfume you're wearing. Perhaps Colly does — suppose we ask him?' And he tried to push past her into the room, then stopped, as he found himself staring into the muzzle of her gun. She said, dangerously: 'I *wouldn't* if I were you.'

He looked at her eyes; she had backed away a step; and the gun was quite steady. He said: 'Showing your true colours, old thing?'

'Never mind about my true colours. Just get along, Dicky.'

He looked at her eyes again; they read the same. If he made any further attempt to see that still figure in the chair, she'd shoot without a second's hesitation!

He shrugged his shoulders.

'All right. Don't waste good ammunition,' he drawled. 'Tell Colly I'll call on him some other time, will you?'

'I doubt if that will be possible. He's leaving the country tonight.'

'He is? Hmm. Too bad. Oh, well, it doesn't matter that much. Good night, Lady Mercia.'

She watched him walk to the lift, saw the doors shut, watched the indicator speeding downwards. She returned into the office, closed the door, and picked up the house 'phone.

'James?'

'Yes, my lady?'

'James, there's a body up here again. I'd like you to move it immediately.'

'Very good, my lady. Who did it belong to?'

'A gentleman named Collwell,' she told him. 'Who meant to sell us all out. I think you'd better mutilate the face a bit before you drop him in the river. Don't leave anything which could serve to identify him, will you?'

'No, my lady. I'll be up at once.'

She laid the telephone aside, sat on the desk again and waited.

The cigarette in Collwell's fingers had

burnt right down, was smouldering against his flesh. His dead eyes stared at her, and through her; a trickle of blood from his head was slowly coursing down his nose, past his open lips, and splattering in tiny drops onto his immaculate evening dress.

There was a knock at the door, and she called: 'Who's that?'

'James, my lady.'

She opened the door for him, and he came in with a large burlap sack. She said: 'Take him into the cellars to do the job on his face, James. Can you manage him alone?'

'George is coming up to help, my lady.'

George, the fat man, entered shortly afterwards. With the body in the sack they moved from the room towards the service elevator. They dumped the corpse in that, and George trotted down to receive it, while James stood guard at the top.

The service elevator groaned and rumbled protestingly at the weight, but at last George called: 'All the way.'

Followed by Mercia, James went to the public lift, and the two shot groundwards.

And Richard, who had returned and

been hiding in Collwell's bedroom, sneaked out, and gave a silent whistle as he made for the stairs!

9

Arsenic . . .

The Chinese restaurant in Soho was practically empty when Lady Standard entered the following night. But over in one corner she could see the unglamorous Cecil, sitting forlornly behind a cup of tea.

She walked over to him, carrying in her hands a little black bag, and he brightened up as he saw her coming.

'Got the dough, lady?'

She nodded.

'Swell. Reckon I'll take it, huh?'

'I'd like to take it myself if you'd be good enough to escort me to Mr. Pagan,' she told him.

'Nerts! Think I'm mug enough to give away our new hidey hole? Get wise, sister. Get wise.'

She shrugged, handed him the bag. 'There it is, then.'

He unsnapped the catch, peered inside.

A smile of gratification crossed his face. 'You done well, lady. We won't bother you none from now on. Now beat it.'

She hesitated. She said: 'I had a proposition to put to your boys, if they're interested . . . '

'They ain't. Take a run, baby.'

She shrugged again and walked to the door; she went right out into the darkness and started down the street. Three yards from the restaurant she cut suddenly into a doorway.

Cecil left a few minutes later, carrying his precious bag. He obviously hadn't considered the idea of being trailed, for he didn't even glance about him. He wasn't very strong on the brain side, wasn't Cecil. He had no idea that a dark shadow slid after him, down tortuous side streets, through the maze of the Soho backwaters, where anything might happen, and often did.

They walked a long way until they were right out of Soho and in a slummy little district near the waterside. The Thames flowed sluggishly past them, a pallid half-moon cutting a silver curve in its black oiliness.

She wondered how long and how far they were going. She was afraid at any minute that Cecil might turn his head and see her. But he didn't. Pleased at having the money, he kept going, never once glancing behind him.

And she kept going after him.

And after her, kept going — Richard Glenning!

It was a case of shadow shadowed. And at last Cecil came to a halt, and Mercia halted behind him, fifty feet behind, and Richard halted in his turn.

Cecil crossed to a shabby little wooden building; what its purpose had been was doubtful; probably the bottom portion had been a boathouse. But it was reasonably isolated, and had two floors. A flight of rough wooden steps ran to the top portion, and Cecil started ascending them. He rapped at the top door two times, then three times, shorter raps. It opened and a dismal glimmer of lamp-light shone out.

He went in and it closed.

The rest of the gang were all there, seated round a rough deal table playing cards. False-face Pagan, looking more miserable than ever, was seated by himself on a bench top near a rusty old circular saw which indicated that this had at one time been a sawmill. He stood up as Cecil entered, said: 'She came tonight?'

Cecil grinned all over his unlovely face, and dumped the bag on the table. There was a simultaneous gasp.

'I told you boys she'd do what she was told,' chuckled False-face, 'didn't I?'

The boys agreed he had.

'And here it is — fifty thousand, isn't it?'

The boys agreed it was.

False-face said: 'Did you look inside, Cecil?'

'Sure I did. You think I'm nerts? I didn't have time to check on it, but there looks like there's one hell of a lot!'

'Good, good. In fact, as I've so often remarked, excellent!'

He unsnapped the bag, glanced down at the neat note stacks. He shut it again.

Harry grunted: 'Okay, let's have it all out, False-face — on the table. Let's cut it up now, huh?'

'No hurry,' Pagan grinned, the twist of his lips turning the grin into almost a grimace of misery. 'No hurry, boys, is there?'

'No hurry be damned,' snorted Harry. 'After what we been through to get that dough there's plenty hurry; yes sir, plenty hurry, and don't you forget it!'

'Where you going?' barked Cecil, suddenly, as False-face turned round and walked towards the door.

'Me? Where am I going? Well, boys, I'm not so sure yet. One can go a lot of places with fifty thousand, can't one?'

'I don't get you,' growled Cecil.

'You don't? No, I shouldn't suppose you did. A man with a skull as thick as yours wouldn't, Cecil. Do you get me, Harry?'

Harry grunted: 'I think maybe I do, Pagan — but you must be haywire. You don't figger we'd let you walk out with our dough, do you?' And he hunched his shoulders and started towards Pagan, his face a mask of savagery.

Pagan snapped: 'Hold it, Harry!'

Harry stared blankly at the revolver his

130

boss held. He held it.

'Pagan — ' began one of the others.

'I know you're wanting to know quite a lot,' admitted Pagan, 'but I can't tell you for the moment. Just stay where you are for a second, will you?'

But ignoring his gun, Cecil started a bull-like rush towards him. Pagan chuckled, and quickly slid outside, slamming the door after him. Cecil hit it, forcibly, gave a roar, and wrenched the handle just as the key turned on the outside. They heard Pagan speaking through the doorway, and they were silent.

'Boys — can you hear me? I expect you can, although the door's rather thick — yes, very thick, boys, just like the rest of this place. We made sure of that when we leased it from old Louie, didn't we? We didn't want anyone busting in and finding our tool kits, our jemmies, our coshes, and our other pleasant little devices, did we? Of course not.'

'Pagan, you rat, we'll kill you for this . . . '

Pagan gave a miserable chuckle. He went on: 'You will? I don't think so, boys. Listen to me carefully. Why do you think I

131

suggested Louie's place as headquarters when we left our old place? You don't know? Well, the fact is I knew this old saw mill was strong. Much too strong for anyone to — break out of, once they were locked in! Then again, it was so constructed that if the bottom floor was set on fire, the fire would spread to the top floor before it had burned through the lower walls. You see, the floorboards are much thinner than the walls, aren't they?

'Yes, boys, that's why I was so insistent on taking the place. I've already soaked the bottom floor with petrol — the second I touch a match to it it'll go up like a keg of gunpowder. And long before it's been noticed, the floor you are standing on will have burnt through, and you'll drop onto the flames beneath! So, on the whole, I don't think you'll kill me, will you?

'Good bye, boys. I'm sorry about this, I really am. But fifty thousand isn't much divided amongst us all, is it? I'm sure you'll agree it's the best way out. Accidental fire; bunch of hoodlums smoking in top of old dry wood mill they used as hideout. Dropped cigarette — POOF!'

They heard his steps descending the stairs; they were petrified into immobility for the moment. They heard the lower door open — seconds passed. Then it was closed again. And below they heard the sudden crackle of the flames, eating at the dry woodwork.

They moved then; there was a tendency to panic, and in their efforts to get to the door simultaneously, they jammed against each other. Already wisps of smoke were beginning to penetrate through the thin floorboards, and grabbing jemmies, chunks of wood, or anything that came to hand, they made an attack on the stout door.

The flames began eating at the boards beneath; charred and blackened sections began to appear under foot. Cecil's leg went right through into flame, and with a scream he drew it up.

Pagan had been clever; there were no windows; the whole affair was excellently constructed; there was no way of getting out at all!

They had to retreat to the far corner, away from the stubborn door; the boards there were caving and cracking. Hysteria reigned among the trapped thugs; they had prided themselves on being able to 'dish it out.' Now they couldn't take it as well!

Now the flames were eating into the woodwork of the room; the place was full of smoke and uncomfortably hot; boards would fall through, and they would have to jump aside. Coughing, half blinded, they staggered about, not knowing which way to turn. Cecil went through the floor into the inferno, with a horrible shriek. Two of the others followed rapidly. Then the entire floor collapsed!

Scream after scream rose from the searing crooks in that blazing mill; but gradually their cries died away . . .

Pagan stood in the shadows outside watching and chuckling. The flames were penetrating through the roof now, and the dense volumes of smoke, mingled with sparks, were attracting the usual crowd. They came from crowded little thoroughfares about the mill, climbing over the dilapidated fence which surrounded it, and regarding the bonfire with exclamations of enjoyment.

The screams of the burning men had been lost in the roar and crackle; and now the clanging of a fire engine sounded along the road, and Pagan decided it was time to go.

He went; Mercia, who had viewed the whole thing from the shadows, dispassionately, followed warily after him; Richard, who had been filled with horror, but had not wanted to show himself, went after her. It was quite a procession!

Pagan walked quickly through the streets; they were filled with queerly assorted people, all hurrying to the scene of the blaze; Pagan chuckled and wondered what they would think when they found the charred corpses of several men in there. Louie could tell the cops he'd hired out his mill to Pagan, of course; but he would naturally assume Pagan had been killed with his thugs in the 'accidental' blaze.

Pagan reached the dirty little house which had belonged to him and his late wife. His late wife had been very late — so late in fact, that when he'd gone for her one night with a bread knife, she'd been too late to stop him. He always had considered it lucky that the river was near, and that people could be mutilated, and that his wife had told the neighbours often that she thought she'd leave him.

He opened the front door, walked in, lit the gas, and set the bag on the table.

Chuckling greedily, he opened it, spilled out the neat piles of bills onto the table top. He started to count, carefully.

His expression suddenly changed; he picked one of the bills up and examined it. He cursed violently.

Snide!

Counterfeit!

'The bitch!' rasped Pagan to himself. 'The cheap, dirty, chiseling, crooked little, dishonest bitch!'

'You talkin' about me, dear man?' drawled Lady Standard from the doorway, and Pagan shot round. He looked at her, then at the gun she held. She came in, shut the door behind her. She said: 'I wondered when you'd find out it was dud money, old thing.'

He started from his chair; she waved him back airily with the gun menacing his midriff.

'Don't get clever, Pagan,' she said lightly. 'I wouldn't hesitate to shoot you, old thing.'

'You twisted little . . . '

She raised her eyebrows, said: 'Pagan! Kindly remember you're speakin' to a lady, will you?'

'Where's the dough?' he rasped at her.

'Ah, yes, the dough, as you so vulgarly put it. The dough is safe and sound where you won't get it. And as for you . . . ' She raised her gun thoughtfully.

He suddenly read death in her eyes, and cringed away. He whined: 'You daren't do that — not here. You'd never get away . . . '

'I'd like to,' she told him. 'Especially after what you did to me. But no matter, you can be useful to me in another way, my dear Pagan. Matter of fact the person I work for needs a new manager for the Satyr Club . . . possibly you'd be suitable?'

He couldn't believe his ears. He gasped: 'Me?'

'Yes, you. As a matter of fact, I had intended to engage all of your boys if they cared to work for me — or rather, I ought to say the person I work for. But unfortunately you seem to have taken care of the others. However, I expect you can make yourself look like a gentleman if you try, and since we're so hard pressed for a good, dishonest man, you'll do, if you're willing.'

'But — how about Collwell?'

'I'd meant to tell you all about Colly, poor chap. He tried to abscond with the profits, and I had to deal with him. You don't think you'd try anything like that, do you?'

'No . . . not if I took the job . . . '

'Either you do, or . . . ?'

He didn't even need to think it over. He'd always envied Collwell his stroke of luck in getting a place as manager of a class joint like the Satyr Club. He said: 'That's Jake by me. If you're on the level, I'm your man.'

'Good. You'll have to cut out those slang terms, you know, and try to speak as a gentleman would. You can — I've heard you, last time we — er — met.'

'Don't worry about that. I can speak

with the best of them. But I'd really meant to move out of town for a time, until this fire business blew over. I'd like the police to think I died in the blaze, if they get to know about me at all. You understand?'

Thoughtfully, she said: 'I know how it is; and I've got just the place for you. You can start at the Satyr in about a month, and meanwhile I'll palm you off on my rich aunt outside town. I can tell her you're a friend of mine suffering from a nervous breakdown, tell her you need peace and quiet. You won't be troubled staying there, and she has plenty of room.'

'How do you know she'd take me?' he queried.

'Don't worry yourself about that. She'll take you all right. But you'll offer her good money for putting you up, see. And you tell her you'll have all your meals outside. She doesn't believe in spending more than she essentially has to, and sometimes she doesn't even believe in spending that amount.'

'I'll do that. Sure this aunt of yours won't suspect?'

'My dear thing, she won't suspect anything. You'd better come along with me, and we'll get a cab to my garage. Then I'll run you down in the car. Better get down tonight; I'm afraid we'll have to knock the old lady up, but that can't be helped. I think the sooner you get out of this district the better.'

'Excellent, excellent,' he chuckled, 'but are you quite certain this person who employs you will want me as manager of the Satyr?'

'Why not?'

He couldn't think of any reason; and if he got the job he thought it would be almost worth losing the fifty thousand for. He'd lost that in any case. He wasn't much use without a gang behind him. He was absolutely helpless with a revolver in *front* of him. He thought it was all rather strange — and he'd have thought it stranger if he could have seen the little bottle marked 'Arsenic,' which nestled in Lady Standard's bag!

10

. . . without Old Lace!

At precisely the same time Lady Standard was removing her car from the garage to motor down to her aunt's, Richard Glenning was tooling his long, sleek, speedy model out of its accommodation.

He had been behind Mercia when she had entered Pagan's home; and he had listened at the door to the murmur of their voices, and had been able to distinguish enough of the conversation to tell him something fishy was afoot. The confirmation of Collwell's death had satisfied him that Mercia was the murderess, and he hoped if he stuck close enough; she would somehow, somewhere, contact the person above her and acquaint that person with the night's events.

He had caught her remarks about taking Pagan along to her aunt's; and remembering what had nearly happened to him down there, he wondered if she were up to some crafty game with Pagan. He could hardly believe, seriously, that the old woman would take in Mercia's story about Pagan being a nervous case; the only way to find anything out was to motor along himself, and see.

Meanwhile, Mercia and Pagan were on their way, whizzing through the downtown traffic, moving perilously fast. For some reason she seemed in a hurry; Pagan wasn't a brave man, and once or twice he caught his breath as she ducked past larger vehicles, and took her chances with the stalwarts of the law.

But at last they were on a straight road which led to the old lady's secluded home, and here Mercia really put her foot through the floorboards.

Half an hour later the house itself came into view, and she swung into the driveway, narrowly missing the corner stones of the double gates.

'Here we are, Pagan, old thing,' she said brightly, dismounting. 'The jolly old aunt's; definitely.'

'I feel a bit silly . . . ' commented Pagan, nervously adjusting his tie.

'Nonsense. Just try and act like a gentleman and you'll be all right. Auntie loves gentlemen. Let's try the bell.'

She grabbed an old fashioned bell pull and tugged. Somewhere in the house a loud peal rang out. They waited. Minutes went by and she tugged again. Pagan said: 'She'll be wild about being disturbed . . . '

'She may be. But it's essential we get you stowed away just in case the police do get suspicious. Here they come now.'

There was a shuffling noise, of carpet slippers, along the passage. A thin voice could be heard grumbling hoarsely. Then the door was opened an inch, but kept on the chain. 'Who's there?' grunted Aunt Abigail.

'Mercia, auntie. Open the door.'

'For Heavens sakes, girl, what do you want down here at this time of night?'

The door opened slowly and the old aunt peered out; her hair was covered by a frowsy nightcap, her aged body was encased in red flannel, beneath which peeped a segment of white flannel. All in all she wasn't an alluring spectacle.

She croaked: 'What's this?'

Mercia pushed her way in.

'Come in, Pagan. This is Mr. Pagan, auntie.'

'And who might he be?' queried the aunt, regarding Pagan with dubious eyes. 'He isn't one of your boyfriends, is he? If he is I must say your taste's going down, my child.'

'No, he isn't exactly a boyfriend, auntie. But he's a good friend of mine, and he's often helped me . . . '

'Helped you? How?'

'Oh, in odd ways,' She said vaguely. 'He's just suffered a severe nervous breakdown, and I thought it would be ever so nice for him to stay with you for a month or two — you've plenty of rooms, haven't you?'

'Yes; but I have to pay for them.'

Pagan put in, quickly: 'That's quite all right, Madam, I assure you. I'm perfectly willing to pay anything you ask.'

'You are, young man? Hmm. Well, don't stand out there in the hall now you've come. Come into the sitting-room.

'Would you guide me, Mercia, dear? My eyes are ever so bad.'

Mercia smiled, took her arm, and guided her into the sitting-room. Pagan followed them. Aunt Abigail said: 'Mercia, dear, what on earth inspired you to bring the fellow along at this time of night? Couldn't you have waited until morning? It's turned eleven.'

'I'm sorry auntie, I keep forgetting you go to bed at eight. Eleven is quite early to us . . .'

'Is it? Well it shouldn't be. It's very naughty of you to stay up until eleven, dear. And if your young friend's going to stay with me until he gets better, he'll have to go to bed at eight sharp. I don't like the idea of the lights and the fire going after eight. It's wasteful, and electricity's a shocking price these days.'

Pagan looked more miserable than usual. His stay with auntie didn't promise to be a very pleasant one. He began to regret his decision to go along there, but it was too late to back out now.

Aunt Abigail said: 'Oh, well, now you're here, I expect you'd like a drink?'

'I don't think I could manage any tea at the moment, Miss Standard, thank you,' said Pagan politely.

'Tea? Who's going to bother making tea at this time of night, young man?' grunted Aunt Abigail. 'I meant whisky.'

'Auntie!' exclaimed Mercia.

'Aha! You didn't know I had whisky, did you young lady? But I always keep a half bottle in, it does me good when I'm feeling very poorly. I keep it hidden away from Esmerelda, if she knew she'd be disgusted — and besides, she might help herself. You wait here, young man, and I'll go and get it. You can't have much — only a sip, but it's good whisky.'

She hobbled off, and Mercia said: 'I'll help her get it, Mr. Pagan.'

Pagan grinned; who'd have thought the old lady kept whisky in the place? Perhaps, after all, his stay wouldn't be so bad. She was a rum old stick on the quiet. He heard the aunt and Mercia coming back; he wiped the grin from his features. They came in carrying the whisky poured out in glasses. There was quite an amount; she hadn't been stingy with it.

And after the events of the night he felt he could do with a good strong drink.

'Here, young fellow, get that down you — it'll warm you a bit, put some life into you.'

She gave him a glass, and he sipped, found it excellent; he said: 'This is really good, Miss Standard. It tastes rather stronger than the usual stuff, I think, but not at all unpleasant.'

'He, he,' chuckled Aunt Abigail. 'It is rather *stronger*, young fellow. Good stuff in it — you wouldn't get *that* anywhere else.'

He drained his glass; passed a hand over his head.

'Did you ever see a play?' questioned the aunt, suddenly. 'With the funny title of 'Arsenic and Old Lace'?'

'Why, yes,' he said. 'I believe I did. Rather a silly plot.'

'That's it. About two sweet old ladies poisoning old gentlemen. Funny, wasn't it?'

'Absurdly funny.' He passed a hand over his forehead. It was damnably hot in that room.

147

'I remember it well,' observed Aunt Abigail; reminiscently. 'It was the last play I ever saw. But, of course, no old lady would poison a person just because she felt they were too lonely to live any longer, would she?'

He was beginning to feel uneasy in the stomach. And uneasy in the mind. He said: 'I — I don't suppose so. No, they wouldn't.'

'But,' she went on. 'They might if they had a good — reason!'

He half rose to his feet; he was aware of the evil grin on the old woman's face; of the smile — the strange smile — the face of her niece.

He suddenly put his hands to his stomach and doubled up with a griping pain; his face went grey.

The old lady chuckled, went on: 'A good reason, Mr. Pagan. Such a reason as I would have for poisoning you — you *were* rather rough with my niece, weren't you? She still has the marks. And she allowed me to see them — you know, I can't have anyone ill-treating people who work for me.'

148

'Then you're — you're — '

'I'm the person they just refer to as 'the old devil',' she told him. 'I *am* an old devil, Mr. Pagan. You found that out, didn't you? Of course, it's rather expensive to put in whisky, but if the whisky is strong enough, people don't notice it until it's down. I have only used it once before — the body is buried in the garden. I don't really mind paying for the whisky though; I like people who come to see me to have something nice to drink!'

She cackled horribly; he was now squirming in agony on the floor, writhing in torment, biting his lips and moaning with the hurt in his inside.

'That's why Mercia brought you down, Mr. Pagan. Not because we wanted you as manager of the Satyr. But because you got in our way. I spent a lot of money on the Satyr, and I intend to make a lot from it. I can't have cheap little nasty men like yourself getting in my way, I really can't. It's too bad. Mercia was going to try to get all your boys down here — but fortunately you took care of the others yourself. Very kind of you, Mr. Pagan.

You'll be seeing them again soon, if it isn't too smoky down there. Won't you?'

She cackled again, pushed his kicking legs away from her feet. She continued: 'With there being only you, that meant you got enough for four or five. I was very liberal with it. You should be grateful, Mr. Pagan. It'll be quick. I could have kept you down here and administered it in your food, but you might have got suspicious. The solution is very difficult to get hold of, but I'm sure you can appreciate it, can't you?'

He was lying doubled up, horrible groans tearing from his lips.

She said: 'He'll be gone in a minute, Mercia. Then we'd better make an effort and get him down under. I wouldn't like Esmerelda to come down tomorrow and find him here. He won't be a pretty sight.'

Mr. Pagan suddenly vomited, violently. Aunt Abigail frowned: 'Oh, dear! Now I shall have to clean the carpet. Really, you'd think the man would have a little more consideration, wouldn't you?'

Mr. Pagan suddenly stopped twitching; Mercia crossed and took a rapid glance at him. She rose; said: 'That's that, auntie. Didn't he hate to go?'

Aunt Abigail chuckled: 'He did, didn't he, my dear? Now we'd better get him into the garden, hadn't we?' Mercia nodded, and showing surprising strength for her age, the old aunt took the legs, and her helpful niece the shoulders. Between them they carried the recumbent Mr. Pagan into the garden, where the same curved moon shone down on the rambling old trees and the matted tangles of high grass.

Mercia brought a spade from the shed, and began to dig hard.

She was strong and supple in spite of her hard nightlife, and the spade sheared through the soft turf with speed and precision. Aunt Abigail said: 'If we have to use this method again, dear, I think we'll weight them and throw them in the small lake.'

'I don't think we need to do it again, auntie,' said Mercia. 'There isn't anyone making a nuisance of themselves at the moment, is there dear?'

'I don't know so much; that young Mr.

Glenning you brought down the other day is getting to be a nuisance, isn't he? You say he's still prying round, my child. Pity that accident with the stone didn't work.'

Mercia looked a little worried. She said: 'I'm beginning to like that man, auntie. I'd hate anything to happen to him.'

'Don't be so silly, child! You mustn't let your heart rule your head, must you?'

'No, I suppose I mustn't. Oh, well. Is this deep enough?'

Looking like one of the witches from Macbeth, the old dame peered into the hole. It was about three feet deep, and five feet long. She said:

'I think so. He isn't a very big man, is he? And when we've replaced the turfs with the long grasses, he'll have quite a green grave, won't he? I don't think we'll offer up a prayer for his soul, my child. I doubt if he had one, don't you? Yes, cover him in now, he'll be quite safe. No one ever comes round here.'

She helped to tuck Mr. Pagan neatly into his little hole. He was quite a nice lit, and apart from a little trouble with his feet they made out quite well. Aunt Abigail looked down thoughtfully:

'It seems such a shame to bury him in those good shoes,' said plaintively. 'I'm sure I could sell them to the milk boy.'

'No, auntie! We mustn't keep anything like that.'

'Very well, my dear. You know best. But it *does* seem a shame.'

Mercia started filling in the grave; Aunt Abigail allowed her gaze to wander round. Mercia said, suddenly: 'Auntie — did you make a noise then?'

'Noise? What kind of noise, my child?'

'As if you'd cracked a twig with your feet?'

Aunt Abigail looked startled. 'No, my dear, I didn't. Did — did you hear something like that?'

'I could have sworn I did. It seemed to come from behind you! From the trees!'

She laid down her spade, the hole filled in. She picked up her bag, extracted the gun from it. There was a sudden stealthy sound of retreat from the trees and bushes behind Aunt Abigail.

Even that semi-deaf lady heard it now. She said: 'Quick, child. You can't let them get away. I'm far too old a woman to hang. I shouldn't like it. Do hurry.'

Mercia plunged recklessly into the trees; the noises were plain now; whoever was in front was moving rapidly. She followed round the house, and burst out onto the front lawn. In the lane a large car was standing, some way down. She began to run towards it, but she was still yards away when it started up, and shot down the road, wildly. She spotted a face peering from the side window, took a snap shot, missed.

The car shot away into the night, and she ran back into the house. Aunt Abigail was already there. Mercia rapped: 'I saw him. It was Glenning, no doubt about it.'

Abigail picked up the telephone, called a number. She said: 'Mercia, what is Glenning's address?'

She told her.

'And you say this young woman — this Sheila Nesbitt, is staying at his flat?'

'I believe she is.'

Aunt Abigail said into the 'phone:

'Hello, is that James at the Satyr Club?'

Mercia tensed.

'It is? Good. This is 'the old devil.' You understand? Good. Listen carefully; I want you to go to the address I am going to give you now. There you will find the Nesbitt girl — you know who I mean . . . ? You are to take her, I don't care how, but get her. Don't harm her, but find a suitable hiding place for her and hold her until you receive my further orders. You will do that *now*, you understand, *at once*.'

She gave the address and laid down the 'phone; she turned to Mercia, said: 'Mercia, you *must* overtake that young man before he gets back to the city. He may go straight to the police, and we can't have that. Tell him we've got his sweetheart, and that if he says anything about this, or attempts to interfere with us, she'll suffer. Make sure he doesn't go to the police immediately, so that we have a little time to deal with him. Meanwhile, I'll remove Mr. Pagan's corpse, just in case. I'll weight it and throw it in the lake. Off you go now, and do hurry!'

155

Mercia nodded, and without waiting to collect her coat, left the house. Her car was standing just within the drive, and she jumped in, revved up.

She swung round almost in her own length, went tearing up the road to London . . . it wasn't a very long journey, and she gradually began to realise she wouldn't be able to catch Richard up before he arrived. As she tore into the outskirts, this became a certainty. However, there was always the chance he would head for his flat, and get the police by telephone. She turned the nose of the car in that direction, and trod savagely on the accelerator.

★   ★   ★

Sheila Nesbitt climbed out of her dress, and stood, for a moment, in her underwear. She thought she had heard a sound at the flat door in the other room. Like someone fitting a key —

Richard, perhaps . . . he was still staying at the Satyr, but he might have come back to tell her something. She knew he was trailing Lady Standard that night, and perhaps . . .

She hastily slipped into a negligee, hurried from the bedroom into the other room. There was no mistake about it; someone was trying the flat door . . . with a key!

It began to open slowly, and she backed away; for the face that appeared there was not that of Richard — but that of James, the steward from the Satyr Club! He advanced right into the room, directed a glance at her, turned and motioned to someone else. The fat man entered.

He was holding a revolver, pointed straight at her. She gasped:

'What — what do you want? What are you doing here?'

Neither of them spoke; James nodded to the fat man. He walked over to her, deliberately. She opened her mouth to scream, and with a speed astonishing in one of his bulk, the fat man jumped forward, with clubbed gun, and brought it down heavily on her head!

The scream was cut off short; she slumped to the floor.

'Think anyone heard it?' queried the fat one.

'I don't think so,' James said. 'Bring the sack.'

'Yes.' The fat man unearthed a sack from beneath his large jacket. Between them they lifted the senseless girl into it.

'We'll get her down the back way,' said James. 'If we're seen we'll just have to knock out whoever sees us. Better be on our guard — this isn't the Satyr Club.'

They hoisted her, and the fat man said: 'You keep your eyes peeled, Jimmy. I can manage her on my shoulder.'

James nodded, and they turned towards the door; and suddenly James thrust the fat man behind the door, and followed himself. Pressed against the wall they waited for the owner of the footsteps they had heard, to go past . . .

11

The Real Lady Standard

Lady Mercia Standard slid her car into the side of road, cut the engine, and climbed out. She glanced upwards, noted the lights in the flat belonging to Richard Glenning. And she also noted, parked close by the entrance, his car.

So he had returned to his flat first; and now, if James and the fat man had done their jobs well, he would be wondering just what had become of Sheila. She entered hastily, found the lift, and shot upwards. She got out at his floor; the passage was silent and seemingly deserted. The door his apartments was slightly ajar.

She began to walk along, cautiously; she didn't wish to burst in too abruptly, there was no telling what the shock might make him do.

She pushed gently at the door; stepped inside — and almost stumbled across the body just inside the doorway.

It was he — Richard Glenning. He was motionless, hardly seeming to breathe. And then a voice spoke behind her:

'It's you, my lady. We thought that it might be someone come to investigate the noise of his fall.'

'James,' she said, spinning round. 'What happened?'

'We were about to leave with the young woman in this sack, when we heard steps. They came in here, and belonged to this gentleman. We took care of him before he had a chance to see us, even.'

'You didn't . . . ?'

'Not that, my lady. He is merely stunned.'

She knelt quickly and examined Richard. He was still breathing, but there was an ugly bruise forming over his right eye. She snapped: 'Did you *have* to hit him so hard?'

James looked puzzled: 'What difference does it make, my lady?'

She stood up; she said: 'It doesn't matter, James, of course it makes no difference. You'd better take the girl now.'

'What are we to do with her?'

160

'Don't harm her — for the time being. You can put her in the cellars at the Satyr Club; use the little cellar off the main wine cellar, and keep her bound and gagged. Lock the door on her, and make quite certain no one goes down there but yourself. Now hurry, before this man recovers.'

They nodded, and James having ascertained that all was clear, they left the room, the fat man carrying the sack.

Lady Standard sat in a chair, lit a cigarette, and watched for Richard to recover . . .

James, the fat man, her aunt, and anyone who knew her baser side, would have been very surprised at the light in her eyes — the glance she directed on his still features — there was no trace of malevolence in it!

Richard Glenning slowly dragged himself from the depths of unconsciousness. He grunted, raised one hand to his head, and then blinked his eyes open. He sipped the whisky which was held to his lips, and became aware of the woman who held it.

'*You!*' he gasped. 'What's happened here . . . ?'

Mercia got up from his side, watched him stagger to his feet. He was still wobbly, and she pushed forward a chair for him. He flopped into it.

'Feel better, old thing?' she drawled, and now that strangely tender look she had bestowed upon him while unconscious, was gone.

He rubbed his temple; then his eyes took in the room. He said: 'Sheila — what's happened to Sheila?'

Lady Mercia lit another cigarette, inhaled and exhaled. 'Sheila? Oh, yes, the young innocent you — er — had at this place. I'm afraid she's — indisposed.'

'What the devil do you mean,' he said angrily, raising himself in the chair. 'If you've hurt her . . . '

'We haven't hurt her, old thing,' said Lady Mercia coolly. 'I see no reason why we should do so, unless you happen to be a stubborn fool.'

'Go on,' he grated. 'Tell me what you're driving at?'

'Well, we've got your precious Sheila. She's quite safe and sound, and more-or-less comfortable at the moment. She will be well fed, and no harm will come to her. Don't try to find her because you'd find it a hopeless task, and we might resent it, and take it out on the girl. Provided you respect our wishes, she'll be perfectly safe.'

'And what are your wishes?'

'Firstly, that you mention nothing of what has happened tonight to the police. Secondly, that you keep your nose out of our business. Two very simple requests.'

'I'm damned if I do — you and that foul aunt of yours'll swing if it's the last thing I ever do, believe me.'

'Really? Aren't you being foolish? I gather you're rather fond of this Sheila Nesbitt, isn't that correct?'

He didn't answer.

'And if you wish to ever see her safe and well again, you'd be silly to communicate with the police. In fact, you'll be signing her death warrant. You've seen my dear aunt in action tonight — you know what she can do — she can also devise some very unpleasant and lingering ways of disposing of a person she dislikes.'

'By God . . . ' he almost shouted, coming to his feet.

Lady Mercia raised a hand in protest: 'Please, Mr. Glenning. Don't exert yourself. It won't do a bit of good. I admit I haven't much of a conscience myself, but it makes even me feel sickly when my aunt talks about ways of murdering people. She likes to kill, especially to kill young folks. She knows she hasn't long to live, and she's infernally jealous of dying, jealous of the people who'll go on living when she's gone. She's very very vicious about it all.'

'I'm not sure who's the worst,' grunted Richard. 'Your aunt or yourself!'

Mercia smiled: 'You wanted to see the real Lady Mercia, didn't you, old thing? You didn't know which was the real one, did you? The polished sophisticate, or the charming frightened girl who begged you to stay away from the police that night? Well, it wasn't either of those two — *now* you see the real Lady Mercia, Richard . . . do you like her any better?'

He wrinkled his nose in disgust. He said: 'I've seen decenter things crawling out of the sewers!'

She didn't take offence; she offered him a cigarette, said: 'I thought you wouldn't like this side of me. But it is the real side. The others were merely acts.'

'I don't like any part of you,' he told her. 'But I'll have to do as you ask. How long do you expect this to go on for?'

'We'll think that over,' she told him. 'Possibly until we've — put you out of the way.'

'You hold life cheap,' he sneered. 'Why didn't you put me out of the way while I was senseless?'

She looked at him thoughtfully. 'You wouldn't understand, I'm afraid. I myself couldn't put you out of the way — nor could I give the order to — I myself would hate to see you murdered!'

'Is this another act?' he said scornfully.

'No, Richard — I don't think it is. I hadn't meant to ask you this, but — well, if I get my pride wounded, I'll have asked for it. There is *another* side to me; and I can't say if it isn't the most sincere side of them all, yet. The other side I've only found lately. I didn't even know I had it.

It's the side of a woman deeply in love.'

'Love?' he sneered. 'You couldn't possibly know the meaning of the word.'

'Couldn't I? Perhaps you're right. But I do know that if you'll agree to throw in your lot with me, say nothing to the police, and forget Sheila Nesbitt, I'll be everything you want in a woman, Richard. I'll do anything you say, I'll see that my aunt accepts you as one of us, I'll try to make you happy.'

'Are you suggesting *marriage*?' he gasped.

'If you want it like that — but personally I think marriage is such an old fashioned institution, don't you? I'm suggesting an alliance — physical and mental. I want you, and if you can bring yourself to want me, we can be very happy — I've told you I'd be anything you wished.'

'There's one thing you could never he,' he snorted. 'And that's *decent*! No, Mercia, I wouldn't have anything to do with a black hearted wretch like you if you were the . . . '

'Don't say the last woman alive,' she

pleaded. 'That's old-fashioned also.'

'Do you think I could possibly live with a woman who might, at any moment, take it into her head to poison my food, or shove a knife through my spine? You're mad! And do you think I could shut my eyes to the things you're doing with that blasted frowsy old aunt of yours, and actually become one of you?'

'You wouldn't have to do anything very wrong,' she told him. 'I was thinking of making you manager of the Satyr . . . '

He laughed without humour. He said: 'Like you did poor Pagan, eh?'

'Pagan deserved to die!'

'Perhaps he did. But you and your aunt aren't qualified to judge. You're both worse than he was.'

'I advise you to think my offer over, Richard. If you fall in with my plan, we'll release the girl, provided you agree not to see or help her again. Otherwise, there's no telling how long we may have to hold her.'

'Don't worry about that,' he snapped. 'The police will soon trace her.'

'I'm afraid, if you inform the police, we

shall be compelled to murder her and dispose of the body. Aunt has already removed Mr. Pagan's corpse to a safer place. The club can be neatly turned into a restaurant in a few minutes, and you would have no evidence to support your charges. I admit you might make things awkward for a time — but it would blow over, and you would be no better off; and the lady you admire so much would be dead.'

She had him at every turn, and he knew it. He was tied; and he could do nothing about anything, in case they harmed Sheila. He knew Mercia would not be above doing that — if, as she claimed, she loved him, she must long to injure the girl *he* loved.

He said: 'Very well. I agree not to tell the police.'

'And — you will fall in with my suggestions?'

He shook his head. He couldn't do that. It would have been like living with some venomous reptile.

She rose from her chair; there was a hurt look, behind her apparently calm gaze. She said: 'I'm very sorry you won't,

168

Richard. It would have solved everything so neatly. Now — we shall just have to arrange to have you killed.'

'You can try,' he told her.

'Think again — I wouldn't be so hard to take, would I?'

She crossed over, sat on the arm of his chair, ignoring his obvious repugnance. She allowed a hand to run through his hair, soothing the throbbing bruise on his temple. Her skirt was pulled taut against her rounded legs, and in spite of his detestation of her, he felt his blood running more quickly. She leaned forward so that the softness of her was pressing hard against his shoulder, so that an insane desire to turn, to reach for her, to thrust his lips fiercely against her smiling, alluring red ones, came upon him. He tried to fight it off, tried to think of what she had done, what she was *likely* to do in the future; but even the remembrance of the hurtling stone she had planned should crash on him didn't help him to resist. His will power snapped, and she was in his arms, lying half across the chair, tempting him with her red lips and slumberous eyes. His own face came down to hers . . .

Then he was lost completely, and even though he felt self-disgust rising in a wave, the perfume of her, the womanliness of her, drowned out his attempts to thrust her aside, and he succumbed.

The world, the universe, was forgotten. He was no longer fighting for Sheila — Mercia was no longer an evil murderess —

Time had stopped, and now they were man and woman, and it was as if nothing else had ever existed.

And at last they broke apart, and she sighed, feeling that he was hers entirely now.

'I'm not so hard to take, am I?' she whispered again.

Mechanically he shook his head; thoughts, other thoughts than those which had occupied him for the brief interlude of passion, were now seeping into his awareness. And on those thoughts he made his decision. He said: 'I think I'm ready to agree to — to your previous proposals.'

She sat up, stared at him.

'You mean that, Richard?'

He nodded.

'If we live together, you'll forget Sheila Nesbitt, how auntie and I make our money?'

'I'll forget everything. But you must release the girl unharmed. She knows nothing about this.'

'Nothing. But you — you aren't tricking me? You won't go to the police later?'

'I give you my word on that.'

'Then we'll see auntie about it. Tomorrow. I'm sure she'll welcome you. We didn't know what to do for a man to run the Satyr, and you have the appearance and the charm needed.'

'How about the girl?'

'Oh, yes, the girl. I can't order her release myself. But it will be all right — she'll be free to go, and she'll come to no harm, provided you keep to your agreement.'

'I'll keep to it. The agreement is that I stay with you, that I don't report what I know to the police, and then I run the Satyr Club for you.'

171

'Yes; that's it. If you give me your word of honour . . . ?'

'Would you accept it?' he smiled.

'I think so.'

'Then you have it. My word of honour I'll respect our agreement. Perhaps you'd like it in a formal contract?'

'No, we needn't go that far,' she replied, smiling. 'I trust you, Richard. And — and — you do love me — a little?'

She looked at him, wistfully. And now he failed to see her as a murderess again — she was just a spoilt, pampered society beauty, in love for the first time in her rotten career.

'Does that matter? If you've got what you wanted, does it make any difference whether you've got something that's sincere?'

'No. I want you badly enough to take you even without your loving me, too. But — I thought — '

'You certainly fascinate me,' he told her. 'And that's as far as I'm prepared to go right now.' He rubbed his temple again, said: 'I think I'd better put something on this . . . '

172

'Let me, Richard . . . '

'Thanks. You'll find the stuff in the bathroom cabinet.'

She hurried to get it, and then, with tender fingers, painted his bruised flesh with iodine.

That done they had a drink, then he yawned: 'I've had rather a heavy day — should be turning in now.'

'Can I — shall I stay?'

He shook his head: 'No, please. I feel a bit seedy from this crack on the head. I'll call you tomorrow morning . . . '

She nodded, kissed him; she said: 'Good night, darling . . . '

12

Woman in a Barrel

Richard Glenning rose early the following morning, and dressed carefully in his best clothes. There was a livid mark on his head from the blow he had sustained the previous night, and he disguised this as much as possible by smearing a little shaving talcum over it.

He breakfasted, and then telephoned Lady Mercia.

Her voice, sleepy and bored answered, but when he made himself known the sleepiness left her.

'Oh, Richard? I'm glad you called dear. Yes, of course we'll go to see auntie immediately after lunch. Will you lunch with me at the Satyr, darling?'

'Certainly,' he told her. 'If I'm sticking to the arrangement we'll be lunching together a great deal in future, won't we?'

'And *breakfasting*, sweet,' she replied.

'Aren't I naughty?'

He controlled the desire to tell her to go to hell, said, instead: 'Yes; won't that be nice?'

'Do you still love me?'

'I still admit you fascinate me.'

'You simply won't say it, will you? All right, darling, you'll learn. Until lunch, then.'

'Until, as you say, lunch!'

'Here's a little kiss for you.'

She made horrible smacking noises over the 'phone, and he put the receiver down with an air of disgust. What a damned actress the woman was, he thought — and what a queer, half repellent charm she could exercise when she chose.

He purposely dismissed the thought of Sheila from his mind; he couldn't help her, she'd be safely hidden away. He wondered if she was at the Satyr Club, or at Mercia's aunt's. He thought it highly improbable. Mercia must know that would be the first place he would look, if he meant to look at all. No, he felt sure Sheila was hidden well away somewhere.

175

He reflected on the previous night's happenings, and a grim smile crossed his face . . .

*   *   *

Sheila Nesbitt lay on a pile of filthy straw cases from old wine bottles, in the small cellar of the Satyr Club, and wondered miserably what would become of her. She had no idea why they had chosen to kidnap, and hold her prisoner. But she guessed it had a lot to do with Richard and his activities. Her face softened as she thought of him; he must be miserable with worry, wondering where she was, and what was happening to her. Or perhaps he had no idea she'd been kidnapped, thought she'd just decided to take a run-out on him.

She shivered a little; it was damp in the cellars, and her negligee had fallen off her during the struggle she had put up when she had come round. Clad only in scanty underthings, the chill was penetrating through into her bones. Nor could she move about to keep warm; she was firmly bound, and gagged.

She wondered dismally how long they'd keep her here, and what they meant to do with her eventually. Something unpleasant she felt sure. Perhaps this had all been instigated by Lady Mercia. She had read the look in that lady's eyes that night when she had broken in upon her and Richard. Mercia, she knew, was in love with Richard — and being a woman herself, Sheila knew how far such a person as Lady Standard was, would go to make sure no one else got the man she wanted.

She was feeling hungry now; since she had been thrown in here by the fat man the previous night, no one had been near her. Once or twice she had thought she had heard movements in the large wine cellar beyond the locked door — but she had been brought no food or drink.

It had been an awful night in the darkness; several times she had felt she would go mad: when the rat had squeaked its furry way across her legs; when she had felt the crawling, unseen insects upon her naked flesh. Loathsome slimy things had squelched their way across her, too; snails, she guessed, but in the dense nothingness, they had made her shudder with horror and revulsion.

She wasn't a particularly squeamish girl; but no girl, squeamish or not, could have stood up to that night without flinching, without sobbing softly now and again. She started as there was the sound of key turning in the lock; the cellar door opened, and James came in. He carried a tray of food, and she watched him lay it down on a rough wine case in the corner.

'I trust you slept well, Miss?' he enquired suavely.

She didn't answer him; she could see no point in discussing anything with him, or in expecting any mercy. His eyes told her she'd get none.

'I brought your breakfast,' he informed her. 'We'll be moving you directly afterwards, so you'd better have a good meal in preparation for the journey. I take it you can eat grilled tomatoes with bacon and kidneys? Or perhaps your night among the furry denizens of this cellar, has spoiled your appetite?'

She'd got past that, however. She ate ravenously with the use of the one arm he had untied, and tried not to show her embarrassment at his glances at her half-clad body. When she had finished he poured her coffee; he said:

'I have had instructions to remove you from this place, Miss. I am not at liberty to inform you where you are being taken, but it will be a little more comfortable.'

'You're afraid,' she said. 'Or whoever directs you is. Afraid Richard Glenning will find me here! Isn't that it?'

He smiled: 'I think you can safely forget Mr. Glenning,' he told her. 'Lady Standard instructed me to tell you, if you mentioned him, the present position of things with regard to that gentleman . . . '

'She — she hasn't — harmed him?'

'On the contrary. She did not actually say so, but I gathered from her remarks that she had been kind enough to bestow her favours upon him.'

She couldn't bring herself to grasp his implication. She said: 'You're a liar — he wouldn't . . . '

'You may believe or not, as you wish.

But Mr. Glenning takes up his duties here as manager — the late Mr. Collwell's position — sometime this week. And since my lady has ordered me to have the top suite, which she ordinarily used with Mr. Collwell, made ready for *two*, I think we can believe only one thing, don't you?'

'He couldn't . . . ' gasped Sheila.

'My lady is a very alluring woman,' observed James. 'There is little any man wouldn't do if she chose to make herself appealing to him. I have murdered men for as much as her smile. What might not other men do, for greater rewards?' And he chuckled lewdly.

Sheila was numbed and shocked by his revelations. She had thought Richard immune from the insidious clutches of Mercia — especially knowing what he did about her. But if this was true, then she could expect no further help from him. She recalled the way he had been clinging to Mercia that night when she had caught them unawares, and she felt suddenly sick and tired.

A great bitterness rose in her against Richard; certainly she had no right to

expect his help, but after his promises
. . . And on top of that she'd really
believed he loved her, as she loved him
— *had* loved him would be a better word.
The news James had brought had driven
all her love away.

James, regarding her from narrowed
eyes, said: 'I see the facts have unsettled
you, Miss? I wouldn't worry about them,
if I were you. There are other, better men,
who could treat you as one so pretty
should be treated . . . ' and he gave an
oily smirk. She shuddered as she looked
at him, at his impassive face which was
belied by the malicious, wanton lights,
which crawled in his eyes like maggots in
rotten apples.

She said, stiffly: 'I'm afraid you're
making a mistake. It doesn't in the least
interest me what Mr. Glenning chooses to
do. He was merely a casual acquaintance.'

'Really? Are you in the habit of staying
at the flats of your casual gentlemen
acquaintances? If so, I have a nice little
place myself,' he chuckled.

She bit her lip and remained silent. A
man like James would never understand

that there could be anything but wrongness in finding her in a bachelor apartment late at night. It was plain he thought she was Richard's mistress — well, let him think. It didn't harm her, and she didn't care what he thought.

There was a light step in the other cellar, and James moved quickly to the door. 'Oh, my lady,' he said. 'The girl is in here as you instructed.'

Mercia entered; she was dressed in a tight dress of some red, clinging stuff, and Sheila could well see how she would infatuate practically any man. She leaned against the door jamb, smoking with a long cigarette holder, and eyeing the half-clad girl vindictively.

'I'm afraid we have to move you,' she said, slowly. 'I'm also afraid the journey will be a trifle irksome — you see, we shall have to resort to camouflage. We have some large beer barrels which are due to go back to the distributors. You will be placed inside one of those, bound and gagged. It will be rather cold for you, attired as you are, but you look rather fetching that way. James thinks so, don't you, James?'

'Very fetching, my lady.'

'And so, you see, we must please James. Has he told you about dear Dicky?'

'Yes,' muttered Sheila.

'Yes? You seem quite upset about it, dear. I shouldn't be if I were you. No man's worth worrying about, I promise you. And in any case you won't live long to worry.'

She cried: 'Richard wouldn't stand for the tricks you get up to . . . he wouldn't allow you to harm me!'

'No, of course he wouldn't. But he *is* getting more sense. He's agreed to take a post as manager here — and he's agreed to be — friendly — towards me, you see. He's labouring under the impression that I shall release you in a month's time, but he's very wrong. You will be released, and promptly. And he will see you go free, don't worry. But he won't speak to you, and you won't have the chance to speak to him.

'He will watch you released from a convenient window, and he will be satisfied. He doesn't wish to see you again, he told me that. What he will be unaware of, will be that before the day is over, you will be killed! Perhaps a rushing motorist, perhaps a quantity of poison, mysteriously in one of your drinks, perhaps a shot in the dark — you will have a pleasant time remembering that, won't you? Wondering where it can be coming from.'

'If I go at once to the police . . . '

'Police? Really, my dear. You've already made a fool of yourself once about this place. And do you think they'd listen again? Especially to wild accusations against Lady Standard? Accusations you couldn't support. You'd be laughed out of the station!'

She laughed, went on: 'Better put her nicely into the beer barrel, now, James, hadn't you? Make sure she's unable to kick at the sides, will you, and that her gag is quite firm. We can't risk any 'accidents.' And by the way, you might have this particular barrel in the rear of the hall in about half an hour, when Richard calls to lunch. There's a small bung hole near the top, and she'll be able to see him — then perhaps she'll believe fully that he's changed a great deal.'

She gave the girl a last, evil look, and tapped out of the cellars.

James re-adjusted the gag and bonds, so that she was unable to stir an inch, unable to make a sound of any description. Then he lifted her roughly, carried her into the wine cellars, and fitted her into a barrel which stood handy. It was a tight fit, and her skin was scraped and grated on the sides, but it was quite dry. As the taunting Mercia had said, there was a small hole near the top, and James fixed her so that she was able to peer through this. Then he slammed down the lid, cutting off all light from her.

It must have been quarter of an hour or so later that she felt the barrel jolted roughly into the air, and knew she was being taken on the start of her journey. They ascended steps, and then the barrel was dumped down again. Now a filtering light entered the tiny hole in the side, and she knew she was at the rear of the hall.

In spite of her desire not to see if what Lady Standard had said was true, she found herself straining to apply her eye to that hole. And finally she succeeded in reaching it, and looking out into the hall.

It was deserted, save for the watchful James, standing beside the barrel. But then the door opened, and Richard — dressed in immaculate clothes, and wearing a pleasant smile — stepped in.

He spoke to a page boy, and then waited. Biting her lip, Sheila watched, unable to tear her eyes away.

Watched, as Mercia walked seductively down the stairs, pulled his face down to hers, and kissed him. Watched him smile at her, watched her slip an arm through his, and prepare to leave.

She turned, called to James: 'Oh, James — you'd better get those over to the warehouse now, hadn't you?'

'Yes, my lady.'

Then they had gone, and Sheila sank back, with a terrible feeling of helplessness and uncertainty.

There was little room for doubt; Richard, whom she had earned to love so much in such a short space of time, had betrayed her!

She felt the barrel jolted up again, heard the clatter of shoes on flagstones, heard the hollow bump as she was dumped into a van. Other barrels clattered against her, ringing painful echoes in her ears, but she hardly heeded them. She was still trying to convince herself that Richard was playing some deep game; but what game? Unless she had thought him sincere, Mercia would never have trusted him. And the way he had received her clinging kiss, as if it was a natural thing!

He hadn't seemed in the least worried about her disappearance. And now he was going to lunch with one of the persons responsible for it, for, as Lady Standard had said, he knew she was being held by her and her thugs.

Endlessly the van rattled on; once it stopped for about ten minutes, and she heard the other barrels being rattled out.

A gruff voice said: 'Yer left one in there, mite!'

James replied: 'No; that isn't for you. That's the lot that you've got.'

'Looks like one of ours?' said the puzzled voice.

'I said it isn't for you! Can't you hear?'

'Awright, awright. Keep yer ruddy 'air on, chum.'

The van started again, moving faster. It travelled this time for about fifteen minutes, and then jerked to a halt.

Her barrel was lifted out conveyed into a building with a wooden floor.

James said: 'This is her. Where'll you have her?'

A male voice answered and then she was carried upstairs. She was released in a comfortably furnished room, without windows, but with ventilators. James said: 'This is another gambling club run by the old devil and my lady. Not as large as the Satyr, but quite profitable. As long as you behave, you'll be treated well here. Carson, the manager, will attend to you. I must leave you now, to get the Satyr Club suite prepared for its new occupants . . .'

The door closed behind him, and the bound girl lay where she had been thrown, and gave way to her grief in low sobs . . .

13

Where's the Body?

The car turned in at the gates of the old fashioned house owned by Mercia's Aunt Abigail. As usual, Esmerelda was waiting on the step to receive a peck on the cheek from Mercia. She looked at Richard as if she thought that possibly he, too, might like to oblige. But no offer forthcoming, she sniffed, said:

'Your auntie isn't too well today, dear. She's in the sitting-room as usual. Go right in, won't you?'

She bustled away towards the kitchen, and Mercia and Richard walked through into the sitting-room.

Aunt Abigail was, as always, sitting knitting. She raised her brows as they entered, said: 'Ah, Mercia, my dear. I received your telegram — you used rather a lot of words — must have been awfully expensive — very naughty of you.'

189

'Don't worry about that, auntie,' said Mercia. 'It isn't every day we manage to secure the services of a gentleman like Mr. Glenning. He'll lend tone to the Satyr Club.'

'Hmm, yes . . . well, sit down, sit down. Make yourselves at home. Take your coat off, young man. I don't like people who come to see me to sit in their things.'

Richard took his coat off; he said: 'I'll keep it handy — I rather like to know I've got a fully loaded revolver handy, you know.'

The old woman raised her brows; she seemed to think he'd struck rather a discordant note. She said: 'We don't talk about things like that in friendly little chats, young man. You mustn't upset me, you know. I haven't been very well today.'

'I shouldn't imagine you have after last night.'

'Hmmph! Well, if you insist on talking about that, I may tell you that Mr. Pagan, in spite of his thinness, was no light weight for an old lady like myself. But I managed . . . I managed . . . ' She gave a horrible cackle.

'Suppose we cut the formalities, and all this beating round the bush, and get down to business?' suggested Richard.

Aunt Abigail glanced at Mercia. 'Your young man is abrupt, dear, isn't he? Almost rude . . . '

'Perhaps we had better get down to business, auntie,' said Mercia soothingly. 'After all, that's why we're here. Mr. Glenning could make things very awkward for us if he cared to . . . '

'And we could make things very awkward for the young lady he thinks such a lot of,' chuckled the old hag.

Richard grunted, said: 'Do you want me for manager of the Satyr, or don't you?'

'But of course we do, don't we auntie dear?' said Mercia.

'I'm not so sure — how do we know you'll play the game with us, young fellow?'

'You don't. But if my word isn't enough . . . we'd better call it all off, and I'll carry on as I was doing.'

'Oh, auntie'll take your word,' urged Mercia, but Aunt Abigail shook her silvery locks.

'I'm not so sure, dear,' she said. 'How do we know this young fellow won't round on us?'

'He could do that now if he meant to, couldn't he?' argued Mercia.

'No; he's afraid of his lady friend being hurt; but if she was released, then there wouldn't be anything to stop him.'

Mercia said: 'Richard, I'd like to speak privately to my aunt for a moment or two . . . if you don't mind.'

'Not at all. I'll hang about outside.'

He went out, closed the door. He heard the low murmur of their voices but could not distinguish what they said . . . he could see right down a long passage, to a door opening onto the rear garden. Swiftly he moved down towards the door, and out into the rank grass.

He found the spot where Mercia had dug the grave for Mr. Pagan, the turfs placed back in position and trodden down flat. And nearby the tall grass was crushed and beat, as if by the passage of some heavy object, dragged across it.

He whistled and began to follow the trail; it led him through a clump of trees, to the side of a small lake, over grown by green scum. The smooth carpet of the greenness, near where the crushed grasses ended at the water's edge, was broken and disturbed as if by something bulky having been thrown into the lake. He tried to peer into the dirty-coloured water, but could see nothing down there.

He murmured to himself, under his breath: 'Ah, well, perhaps it's as good a place as any for you, Mr. Pagan. You'll feel at home with other slimy beings, I expect.'

He turned towards the house, followed the crushed trail back again . . . he looked towards the rear door . . .

'Don't you think my garden's beautiful?' cackled Aunt Abigail, staring piercingly at him from the shelter of the small porch.

He decided to bluff it out. He said: 'You shoved Pagan back in the woods somewhere?'

'Did we?'

'I think it was the best place for him. No one would think of digging amongst all those trees.'

He wondered if he'd fooled her, was aware of her eyes boring into him like gimlets, and felt relieved as she said: 'Among the *trees?* Did you find the exact spot, young man?'

'No; I couldn't seem to locate any freshly turned earth.'

'Just as well, just as well. Mercia's looking for you in the front garden. We've reached an arrangement.'

'Fine. What is it?'

'Better come along inside. Mercia will tell you.'

They walked back into the house; she watched him carefully, said, as they entered the sitting-room: 'Mercia tells me you and she are — what shall we say? — in love with each other? Is that right?'

'She fascinates me,' he told her.

That seemed to satisfy the old lady. She went on: 'I think it's high time Mercia had a man of her own — someone she could count on. She explained to me that you and she would occupy the suite at the Satyr?'

'That's so.'

Mercia came in at that moment. She said: 'Oh, you found him. Well, Dicky, it's all right. Auntie's listened to reason, and

194

she thinks the idea a good one.'

'Excellent idea,' agreed the old woman. 'There's just one little thing, and I'm sure neither of you will mind it. It's just that I'm an old woman, and I don't like modern ways. I don't like people to have loose morals. So you must be married!'

'*Married?*' It was a simultaneous cry from Mercia and Richard. The old dame nodded.

'I said married. I know you carried on with Collwell, Mercia, but I decided then it would be the last time I'd put up with lax morality beneath any establishment I owned.'

Richard grunted: 'You aren't so principled yourself, are you?'

'That has nothing to do with it, young man. If I were young I should never propose to live as Mercia has done. She should be married — she must have children. Or who will all this money we've made go to? Besides, if you love her you'll want to marry her!'

'But aunt, I don't want to be married,' said Mercia, stubbornly. 'I wouldn't be happy.'

'There's another thing,' cackled the old lady. 'And that is that *a man can't testify against his own wife!* Now do you see what I mean? If Richard means to really join us, he'll make no objections to marrying you, my dear. And if you tire of each other, later, well, you'll be able to think of something, I'm sure!'

Mercia realised her cunning old aunt was right. She glanced at Richard questioningly. She said: 'You agree to that, Richard?'

He didn't hesitate. He said: 'Yes, I agree.'

The old lady rubbed her hands. 'I'll make you a nice wedding present — a fish slice! Won't that be nice? Heh, heh, heh. Mercia won't ever use it of course, but it'll be so inexpensive. Gifts are so dear these days.'

'How about the girl — Sheila Nesbitt?' demanded Richard.

'How about her? If you love Mercia, it doesn't matter what happens to her, does it?'

'It certainly does. I refuse to let any innocent person suffer. You'll have to take

196

me on those conditions, or not at all.'

'We've arranged, all that,' said Mercia, hurriedly. 'Sheila will be released a month from today . . . you'll be able to see her go free. Will that satisfy you?'

'A month? Why that?'

'It's a kind of probationary period for you,' said Aunt Abigail, reasonably. 'If you live up to our expectations in that month, we'll let the girl go free. If not . . . '

Richard nodded. He said: 'In that case, I'll marry Mercia the minute I see Sheila released — not before. How's that? That's a kind of probationary period for *you!*'

'You *are* a determined young fellow,' wheezed Aunt Abigail. 'I think you'll be very useful to us if you obey orders. How much will you expect from the takings of the club, as your salary?'

'I won't expect a thing,' he told her, and noticed the gratified gleam in her eye. 'I've got plenty of money. I'm taking the job because it ties in with Mercia's life, so I'll be able to be near her continually.'

'Excellent, young fellow. I like you more than ever with each passing minute. But understand this: unless you marry

Mercia at once, I won't sanction any living together! If you insist on waiting until the Nesbitt girl is released, you must behave.'

'I give my word on that, too,' agreed Richard, and saw the annoyed look in Mercia's eyes.

Mercia pouted: 'That's silly, auntie . . . '

'I don't care. I won't have you carrying on. If you don't like it you must marry now.'

'Sorry,' Richard said. 'Not until the girl's released.'

Mercia looked sullen, and glared at him, but let it drop. The old woman said: 'And if you betray us, young fellow, be sure you won't live long enough to gloat over it. You'll be watched every minute of this month. Every second. You may not be able to see your watchers, but they'll be there.'

'I've given my word,' he grunted. 'That stands.'

She hobbled across to the sideboard. She said: 'Let's have a drop of what made Granny stagger — heh, heh, heh. Sort of clinch the bargain, eh, young roan?'

She poured whisky, offered him a glass. He grinned. 'Do you think I'm stupid?'

'Eh?'

'Think I want to join Pagan?'

'Oh, I see. You're frightened.'

'As frightened as hell,' he said frankly. 'I wouldn't touch any of that stuff unless I was absolutely certain it was okay.'

She cackled and held the glass to Mercia. She said: 'Your young fellow thinks I'm Lucretia Borgia, dear. Show him it's all right!'

Mercia said: 'Is it?'

'Good gracious me, of course it is. Do you think I'd poison you, my child?'

'I wouldn't put it past you, auntie. But all right.'

Richard couldn't restrain a chuckle. They were both so deep in evil that they couldn't even trust each other. He knew they'd keep their words and have him watched for any false moves. He didn't mean to make any. It was arranged that he should commence his duties at the Satyr Club the following Monday. And with that arrangement they took their leave, leaving old Aunt Abigail waving them goodbye from the window, looking every inch the dear old lady, and wiping an imaginary tear from her eye as they roared off into the road.

★　★　★

Richard found his duties at the Satyr Club extremely light. As long as he stood round and looked pretty, as long as he stowed the takings safely away in the safe, as long as he didn't try to get out alone, he was all right.

But once or twice when he went out by himself, he was aware of shadows; shadows which hung onto him like leeches, and which he made absolutely no attempt to ditch. It wouldn't have been wise. He had to play the game straight if he wished to save his own skin.

The weeks slid by, and although Mercia occupied the top suite at the club, he didn't go anywhere near her, preferring to occupy a small room on the lower floor. Apparently she was satisfied with him, in every respect bar one. And towards the end of the fourth week, she drew him aside one night.

'Dicky — what's come over you? You didn't act this way at your flat that night. Why start now?'

'I don't understand, Mercia? What are you driving at?'

She pouted: 'You know very well. The way you've been these last few weeks. Why don't you come and stay with me?'

'Sorry. I gave my word to the old devil — and I won't break it. I keep my promises.'

'But it doesn't matter about this one . . . and in a few days we'll be married.'

He said: 'I'm not anticipating anything, so don't worry me. I've quite enough work to do here.'

She walked away, sulkily.

Each weekend, the manager of another of the gambling clubs brought the takings of his place over to the Satyr, so that they could be lumped together, and handed over to Mercia. It was part of Richard's work to attend to the counting and bookkeeping, and this Saturday was no exception. Carson — whom Richard found rather an inoffensive man, brought the bag round with the takings, and left it with Richard. Richard sat up late, undid the wads of notes, and laid them neatly on the table, preparatory to counting them.

His eyes became fixed on something white in the first pile; far too white to be a note. He unsnapped the rubber band, slid out a thin piece of paper. As he read it his face grew dark, and he uttered a loud curse.

Dear Mr. Glenning,

I am being held prisoner at the other club, run by a man called Carson. I know that you are now working for Lady Standard, and that you are a good friend of hers. But I don't believe you know what they plan to do with me, after you have seen me released. They intend to murder me!

Lady Standard herself told me that, and I understand from her that you do not know.

I am endeavouring to get this note to you; the safe in which Carson keeps all the club money is in the room where I am imprisoned. I overheard him saying that he takes the money to the manager of the Satyr Club every week, and since I know you are now that person, I have taken the chance of writing this message, and slipping it in his stack of notes while his back was turned. If I am successful, you will receive this, and know how things are.

You may, of course, not care what happens to me anymore; if that is so, I should prefer you to keep all this quiet.

Many thanks for your help in the past,
Sheila Nesbitt

He crumpled the note thoughtfully, set a match to it, and saw it flare up. His jaw was set hard — his eyes were grim . . .

So Sheila was at the other club? And they intended to kill her? And *tomorrow* she was to be released . . .

14

Release for Sheila

Early the following morning, Richard Glenning left the Satyr Club, and proceeded towards Piccadilly. He wandered aimlessly for a time, then walked into a second-hand bookshop, and began to turn over the old volumes there.

He was aware of James, close behind him; James or the fat man never let him out of their sight for a moment. The telephone at the club was always guarded, so that if he made — or started to make — a call from his own room, it was picked up on the extension 'phone.

He had also been warned against posting letters; that would have meant trouble, and at present Mercia had to look over every letter he wished to send. But he had agreed to all these arrangements; 'the old devil' meant to take no chances, and he was willing to fall in with any precautions she considered necessary to prevent him contacting the police.

Possibly, in time, when they could be sure of him, the spying would be discarded; but until then he just had to endure it silently.

James took up a position inside the doorway, watched, lynx-eyed, as Richard thumbed through old editions. Finally Richard selected one, took it to the shopkeeper.

'How much?' he enquired.

It was a bulky volume, and the shopkeeper said: 'What is it, sir?'

'Old edition of Dickens,' Richard told him. 'The date's on the second page, here . . . ' He skimmed over the fly-leaf, pointed.

The shopkeeper peered, adjusted his glasses, and peered again. He opened his mouth to say something, and Richard said, quickly: 'If you haven't set a price, suppose we say — three guineas? I doubt if you'd get any more for it.'

'Why — er — no, I shouldn't, sir. That will be excellent. Will you take it along with you?'

'I don't think so. I'm lunching out, but if you'd see that it gets sent over to the

Satyr Club in Mayfair, immediately, I'd be much obliged.'

'Certainly sir. Immediately, you say?'

'Please. I'd rather like to glance through it today. I've been looking for this particular edition for some time.'

The shopkeeper made a note of the address.

Richard said: 'You won't let me down, will you?'

'Rely on me, sir. I'll attend to the matter right away.'

'Good.'

Followed by the watchful James, Richard went out. His arrangements were to meet Mercia for lunch at one-thirty, and then, Mercia had told him, she would take him round to see Sheila being released. She knew nothing of the note he had received from Sheila, and she thought he was still labouring under the belief that once the girl was released the matter was ended as far as he was concerned. But at lunch he suddenly said: 'I've been thinking. About Sheila Nesbitt.'

A trace of annoyance showed itself in Mercia's face. She said: 'You have? Why?'

'It just struck me that perhaps you're

playing some funny game, that's all. Suppose, for instance, when you've let the kid go, you set your thugs after her?'

'I've given you my word,' said Mercia. 'You must trust me. I've taken your word, haven't I?'

'Have you? If that's so, why does James follow me all over?'

'That isn't by my orders. It's auntie's idea.'

'I see. Well, suppose *auntie* intends to have the girl killed.'

'She wouldn't.'

He let the matter drop; after all, it wouldn't do to rouse her anger by thrashing it out any more. He only hoped that his scheme would work out, and so ensure, if nothing else, Sheila's safety.

Mercia said: 'You promised we'd be married as soon as the girl was turned loose. Does that still hold?'

'Naturally. We'll be married the minute I can get the license through.'

'I've got it, Richard. We can be married today.'

'What's the hurry?' he frowned. 'Are you up to something again?'

'No; why do you think I am?'

'You seem so anxious to rush things. Anyhow I won't go through with it at once; tomorrow morning will do.'

She nodded resignedly. She'd found out he could be very stubborn and during the short period he'd been at the club, she'd ached for him terribly. But he had never so much as embraced her properly since he had given his word not to live with her until after the girl was free and they had been married.

She contrived to get James alone before they left for the club Carson ran, in which Sheila was imprisoned. James said: 'I'm to carry out the plan as arranged, my lady?'

'Yes, James. Carson, acting on my instructions, administered a drug to the girl last night. She'll still be hazy this morning, and when she's turned loose, your job is to be waiting round a handy corner with the car — you attached false number plates?'

'Yes, my lady.'

'You know what to do then; follow her until she is some distance away from the club, and then run her down. Make sure you hit her *hard*, James, and get clear yourself. Carson has removed all identifying marks, and since her father and mother are already dead, it is likely the police will be unable to trace her.'

James nodded and took his leave, and Mercia joined Richard who was waiting outside in the car. Richard said: 'Where is she?'

'Matter of fact she's at Carson's club — you'll be rather surprised to learn she was so close, won't you?'

'I am,' agreed Richard, successfully portraying surprise. They moved into the traffic, shot down the Strand, turned right, towards Carson's club. It was similar to the Satyr Club, except that it had spacious grounds, a long drive, and the house was smaller. Richard was shown in, and he and Mercia took positions in the front window. Mercia said: 'All right, Carson, you can turn her free, now.'

'Mind if I have a word with her?' asked Richard.

'I *do*,' said Mercia emphatically. 'That wasn't in our arrangement. I'd prefer you didn't see her.'

'But why?' he insisted.

'Why? Well, I'm afraid you must put it down to sheer jealousy. I'm worried in case the old spark still lingers — you see?'

He grunted and turned towards the window. Behind his back she cast a malicious smile at him. Little did he know his precious Sheila would be dead within the hour — if James performed his job properly.

Richard stiffened, suddenly; a girl had appeared from the rear of the house; she walked a little uncertainly, drunkenly. She was garbed in ill-fitting black dress, and black suede shoes. As she negotiated the driveway, she lurched a little.

Richard snapped: 'Are you sure she's all right? She looks as if she's been drugged or doped to me.'

'What if she has? That's only so she won't know where the location of the club is. It will wear off.'

'You mean it's some stuff to make her forget what's been happening to her?'

'That's all.'

Meanwhile, Sheila, dazed and listless, walked along the drive into the roadway.

The drug they had used had wiped away all her memories; things were dim and vague, she couldn't recall where she'd been or what she'd been doing, nor where she was going now. It was an effort even to walk steadily but she turned along the long, tree lined road, started trudging towards a distant main street. She turned a corner, not knowing, and not caring, where it might lead her. And at the far end of the road she had just left, James grinned evilly, started up the long sleek car with which he was to murder her!

But another car passed him even as he pushed in his gears; it turned into the road she had taken; and when James rounded the corner he was just in time to see two men forcing the girl into their car, roughly. They jumped in after her, the car roared to life, and shot away down the road.

Paralysed, James stopped.

Who they were, what they wanted with her, he had no idea. But the way they had spirited her away like that seemed to argue they could not have been merely offering her a lift out of kindness. No, someone else must have it in for Sheila Nesbitt!

Thoughtfully he turned his car, headed back to the Carson club . . .

★   ★   ★

Aunt Abigail sighed and laid aside her knitting. She stared at the figure alighting from the car outside her home. It was James, and James meant trouble. Mercia never sent him down unless something had gone amiss. What had happened now, she wondered? Things were all going wrong, lately.

Esmerelda, who, to give her her due, had no idea what a wicked old woman she was keeping company, escorted James in. She was all of a flutter, for she understood that James was a distant cousin of Abigail's, and as his visits were so few and far between she felt sure her mistress would be pleased.

'Mr. James Corgate,' she bubbled. 'And shall I put eggs on, Abigail?'

'No,' snapped that lady. 'Just leave us alone, Esme. I'll let you know if I need anything.'

James had sat down opposite her, and

now, as Esmerelda closed the sitting-room door, Abigail wheezed: 'Well, what is it? What's gone wrong now?'

'My lady sent me down,' he told her. 'It's the Nesbitt girl . . . '

'The Nesbitt girl? What's happened there?'

'I was prepared to run her down as directed,' stated James, stiffly. 'I had the car in position for doing so, but when I turned the corner, the girl was being forced into another car which had followed her. They drove away.'

'Where to?' hissed the old woman.

'Where to . . . ? I — I don't know . . . '

'What? You fool, didn't you *follow*?'

'I hadn't thought . . . ' he stuttered.

'*Bah!*' cursed the old woman. 'What *dolts* I employ!'

'I didn't think it was essential,' he explained. 'I took it for granted that someone else must wish her harm — and the car moved too rapidly for me to think properly.'

'Pah! If it had moved at a snail's pace you still wouldn't have had time to think properly, at the rate you think! You idiot! Don't you see?'

'See what?'

'What's behind this — I feel sure of it! Only Mercia, myself, yourself, Carson, and Richard Glenning knew that girl was to be freed. Yet someone was waiting — Mercia and I can be eliminated — and I know yourself and Carson would never betray me. So that, if anyone could have had a hand in this, it must be Glenning. He must have suspected that we'd try to kill her, later . . . '

James started, said: 'But how could he have got word to anyone? He's been watched every second as you instructed.'

She shook her head. 'I don't know that — but it's happened. He must be put out of the way, and we must find that girl and get rid of her, also. Listen — tell Lady Mercia nothing of the orders I am going to give to you now; carry them out yourself, and keep the entire matter to yourself.'

'Yes, Madam.'

'First of all you must dispose of Richard Glenning. I don't care how, as long as it looks like accidental death. Mercia will suspect, but she cannot be sure. She would be annoyed, very; if she knew I had ordered his death. Then you must not rest until the girl has been traced and murdered. It is the only way we can be safe. You will get rid of Glenning tonight . . . without fail . . . '

James nodded: 'I understand.'

'You have a plan?'

'Yes, Madam. I will persuade him to come up onto the flat roof of the club — it will be easy to tell him there is something there which merits his attention. Once near the edge of the roof I will push him over — quite a long, and a hard fall, onto solid concrete.'

'Good. Then you had better get back, James, and attend to that.'

He nodded and picked up his cap. She said: 'There will be a good bonus for you, James, if you carry out my orders quickly and efficiently.'

She watched him leaving, watched his car roar away towards London itself. Then she relaxed with a gloating chuckle. If anyone could get Glenning out of the way it was James.

Esmerelda suddenly hurried in, greatly

agitated. She gasped: 'Abigail — Oh, Miss Abigail — there's some strange men in the garden, near the lake. I caught a glimpse of them through the back kitchen window!'

'*What?*'

Abigail came to her feet, her eyes staring from her head.

'By the *lake*, Esme?'

'Yes, Miss Abigail. Awful, rough looking men. I'm so afraid. We really shouldn't live here alone, two defenceless old ladies.'

Aunt Abigail smiled, a mirthless smile. She snapped: 'You'll find a revolver in a little drawer in that desk — hand it to me!'

'*Miss Abby!*'

'Hand it to me, woman! We have a right to protect ourselves and our property, haven't we? I shall only use it to threaten them with!'

Dazedly Esme did as she was told, handling the gun with horror-wide eyes. Abigail caught up her rusty black skirts, rustled down the passage, into the garden . . . Esme followed her, bewilderedly, through the trees towards the lake . . .

There were, as Esme had said, rough looking men there. About ten of them — including uniformed constables!

Abigail stopped with a hoarse cry; for they had hold of grappling hooks, and their operations had just finished!

Beside the grappling hooks, dragged from the disturbed slime of the lake, was Mr. Pagan! Beside him, water wasted, was another gentleman she had once disposed of! The men turned and saw her; and one of them said: 'Arrest her, constable . . . that's the woman. We have all the evidence we need in Richard Glenning's statement!'

Aunt Abigail rapped: 'Stand where you are — the first man to stir gets a shot through him.'

She meant it; the first speaker said: 'All right, you men. Don't ask for it — the game's up for her anyway. An old woman can't skip the country so easily.'

She grated: 'I can try, gentlemen. I can try — and if I am to be taken, I would very much like to see Mr. Glenning before I allow my capture to take place.'

She was backing away, backing towards the house. It was a last mad stand for freedom, which couldn't possibly succeed. And Esme, meek, timid, gushing Esmerelda, who had stood entranced all this time, now realised fully the mistress she had served. With a thin shriek she threw her arm forward, knocked the revolver up in the air . . .

The constables rushed forward.

Aunt Abigail cackled insanely; it was the end, the absolute end. The revolver was reversed; her eyes glared as they drew nearer; and she pulled the trigger with an exultant laugh!

The bullet entered her brain; she knew the spot, knew which point would bring death at once.

She didn't mean to suffer like her victims. She was dead before she had fallen to the soft turf . . .

And Esmerelda, with a loud, expiring shriek, fainted.

'By God, what an old devil,' grunted Chief Inspector Craig, of the Yard. 'Could anyone imagine an old thing like that getting up to such diabolical stunts?

Thanks to Glenning we've found her out at last — I'm sorry she'd got the gun though. If ever a woman deserved to hang, it was her.'

One of the constables found a piece of canvas, covered up the old lady's body. She looked quite sweet in death. Her eyelids had closed over the mad glaring eyes, and her features had straightened out, calm and serene. But there was a cynical twist of the lips — a twist which made it seem that she was laughing, sneering, at the men who had failed to trap her.

They left her there. There was much yet to do. Glenning's instructions, which they had at first assumed a practical joke, had been proved valuable, and authentic. Carson — a man called Carson who ran a gambling club, that was their next stop!

★   ★   ★

Carson smiled politely at the guests who streamed past him into the club. The gamblers were already crowding the boards, and more arrived every minute.

219

His club was not quite so elite as the Satyr; but the men who did come there, if not actual society, had plenty of money to throw away, and Carson got a fine rake-off from the takings.

More of them; a party of about six, walking along the drive.

There was an altercation with the doorman. He appealed to Carson.

'These gentlemen wish to come in, sir, but they have no entry cards.'

'I'm sorry, gentlemen,' Carson smiled, suavely. 'This is a private club, I'm afraid. Perhaps if you have friends already members to vouch for you, something can be done . . . '

'Something *will* be done without that,' grunted Craig of the Yard. 'We have information this is a private club — but not such an innocent affair as billiards, booze, and back-scratching. We have reason to believe it's *a gambling club*!'

'Who are you?' stammered Carson.

'Scotland Yard!' snapped Craig, Carson reached for the alarm bell, but his arm was caught before he even got near it. The police had surprised him very neatly . . .

15

Lady Standard Steps In

Mercia Standard looked round the crowded gaming rooms, and then linked a possessive arm in Richard's.

'Everything's all right now, Dicky?' she said. 'You're quite satisfied now we've released Sheila Nesbitt?'

'I think so . . . '

'And tomorrow . . . ' she went on, giving him a smile.

He didn't reply; he had things on his conscience. Of course, he owed no loyalty to the woman by his side, who had murdered and lied and cheated; and yet he felt strangely sorry for her; within half an hour her little world was to crash to pieces; within a half hour she would be in the hands of the police, and her only possible end could be the gallows.

He glanced at his watch; the police, if they had obeyed his instructions, would now be raiding Carson's club.

But — perhaps they hadn't even received his letter!

Perhaps the bookseller had regarded it as a joke; he tried to put himself in the man's position — he had written the letter in his rooms, the previous night. He had taken it with him, and when he had skimmed through the edition of Dickens, he had slipped it in between cover and flyleaf. The top line had read: 'I am watched. Act as if nothing unusual was happening. Deliver the enclosed letter to the police at once, and insist that they act upon it.'

The bookseller had seemed a sensible sort of chap; and that first glance he had seemed to understand. Anyway, he had played up so that James had suspected nothing.

The letter had given brief but explicit details; the police were first to rescue Sheila, to pick her up soon after she had left the club, and keep her out of harm's way until the gang had been rounded up.

Next, he had instructed them where they might discover the body and the murderer of one Mr. Pagan.

Thirdly, he had laid bare the details about the club run by Carson, and lastly, about the Satyr Club.

If they had the sense they could nab the whole gang; and now that the time drew near for their entry into the Satyr, he was uneasy in case they had slipped up.

He excused himself from Mercia, suddenly; she watched him walking across the room, towards the gentlemen's cloakroom. She transferred her attention to the gaming tables.

He dodged rapidly behind the curtains which led to the rear stairs, used only in the event of a police raid, for the clients to escape. He moved down these, found the rear door.

Quickly he shot the bolts, making as little noise as possible. Then, the way open, he returned to the rooms above. If the police worked to his schedule, they would enter by that door in about ten to fifteen minutes. The surprise would be complete.

Mercia was where he had left her; she had not noticed his activities.

James was standing nearby, and as Richard returned, he cut across and said: 'Mr. Glenning, could you spare a minute?'

'What's the trouble?'

'It's on the roof, sir. Apparently one of the gamblers who has lost too much has gone up there and killed himself. Stabbed himself, to be exact.'

'What?'

'It often happens, sir. We have to get rid of the bodies as best we can . . . '

Richard paused, uncertainly. He had no desire to leave the room now the raid was so close. But he did not wish to rouse suspicion.

The matter was taken out of his hands; there was a patter of steps from the rear of the room, and a loud voice boomed:

'*This is a police raid. Stay where you are, everybody!*'

Immediately there were panic stricken cries. People started to rush wildly towards the other exit, jammed in the doorway in a kicking, struggling mass. Many of them had reputations to uphold, which would have been ruined by being caught in such a place.

Stout politicians hacked the shins of Dukes; Duchesses fought tooth and nail with kept women. Turmoil reigned.

And as Richard spun round to get hold of James, that worthy started to run.

The mass in the doorway suddenly burst, and caved through, in a yelling body. James went with them.

Richard let him go; he was aware that the police would have the place surrounded. No one could get out or in.

A burly, red-faced man strode over towards him: 'Mr. Glenning?'

'Yes, that's me.'

'Good. We followed your instructions to the letter. We thought it might have been a practical joke at first; but events proved us wrong.'

'You saved the girl?'

'Yes, I sent two men along to pick her up the moment she left the Carson Club. She was a bit too doped to tell us anything at the time.'

'And the old woman?'

'Shot herself. We couldn't stop her in time.'

There was a low cry from behind him. He turned; Mercia was held in the strong grasp of a police constable. Her eyes held no bitterness — only sadness and reproach, as they looked at him.

'Richard — you — you broke your word!'

'I'm sorry,' he told her, and meant it. 'But what else could I do?'

'You — you didn't — you didn't love me, then? Never?'

'I never said I did. I admitted you fascinated me, but that was all.'

'And you never intended to join us?'

'I'm afraid not. I only played you along until I was able to get Sheila safe — I undertook to help her to trace her father's murderers, and I've thought of nothing else since, but how I could do that. This was the best way to net all of you.'

She said: 'But you didn't get her father's killer — James did that, and he isn't here! I saw him escape with the crowd!'

The Chief Inspector butted in: 'In that case, he'll be in custody downstairs. We have the place surrounded!'

Down below the police were busy taking names and addresses. Most of the patrons were permitted to go home after that formality, and eventually the only ones left were the police, Richard, Mercia, and the club staff.

Of the elusive James there was no sign.

'He can't have escaped, sir,' said a puzzled Sergeant. 'We had a chain of men all around the place, hands joined. No one got past them.'

'Better search the building,' Craig told him. 'Try the cellars and the roof. I'll get this lot off to the station.'

Hastily, constables were detailed off to make the search. Then the staff, and Mercia, were marched into the drive, where a Black Maria was waiting. Richard crossed to the Inspector, said: 'I'd like a word with Lady Standard, if you don't mind.'

'Private?'

'If it can be managed.'

The officer looked dubious. But eventually he said: 'Well, I suppose that's the least we can do for you, eh? Very well.'

He turned to the man who held

Mercia: 'Walker — allow the young lady to have a word in confidence with Mr. Glenning. You can watch her from a few feet away.'

Mercia walked slowly to where Richard stood, his back to the house. She stood in front of him, silently. He said: 'Mercia, I know what you must think of me — I had to break my word — and I'm afraid I still believe I did right. But I'd like to tell you that if things had been different . . . '

She laughed, scornfully. She said: 'You don't have to apologise, Mr. Glenning. Not at all, old thing; you, as you say, did right; but definitely!' She lit herself a cigarette, blew smoke into his face. 'You blasted swine!' she added, in a low voice.

He shrugged, unable to think of a reply . . .

Meanwhile, up on the roof where he had fled, James was leaning over the parapet, his eyes glazed and wild. He knew what was coming to him; and Richard Glenning had caused it all! He couldn't make an escape, now; but if he was to hang he might as well hang for Glenning as well!

He could hear steps below him; the constables must be searching. In a few seconds they would reach him up there, and his chance would be gone. He eased his hand into his jacket pocket, drew out a small revolver. He levelled it at the garden below . . .

Glenning was down there, plainly visible in the moonlight; he was talking to my lady, doubtless gloating over the way he had tricked her. The Maria stood nearby, ready to take its cargo of cutthroats to prison, and execution. His friend, the fat man, was peering from the barred window . . .

He fitted his finger round the trigger.

Mercia's eyes, glancing round disdainfully, saw his face peering over the edge of the roof; and the gun in his hand . . .

An expression of triumph crossed her face; her heart leapt exultantly; Sheila Nesbitt wouldn't have him, after all; no one would have him. He would be as dead as she was shortly to be!

What strange emotions surged in her breast, cannot be told.

But at the end Mercia went a long way

towards redeeming herself.

For the vengeful spasm passed almost at once; her eyes took in Richard, his tall suppleness, his firm mouth against which she longed still to press her own lips; his sturdy shoulders, and the contrite way he had apologised, even to a woman like herself, for breaking his word.

And as James shot his hand forward, and pulled the trigger, she moved forward, suddenly . . . Richard was pushed out of the way; she stood where he had been. The bullet ploughed viciously into her breast . . .

Love had triumphed over vengeance; and if it was the only decent action she had ever done, it was all the more wonderful for that. And as she sank to the concrete surround of the house, the police burst onto the roof behind James — wildly he fired the remaining shots in his revolver, and with a last, fierce, desperation, he jumped from the edge of the roof he had intended to push Richard from.

He landed only a few yards from Mercia; his head cracked neatly, with sufficient force to kill him instantly.

But Richard paid no heed; in the center of a crowd of police officers, he knelt, raised Mercia in his arms. Her face was very white, her evening gown was stained with red. Her eyes were dimming rapidly, and her breath whistled into her throat.

'Had to — do — it,' she whispered, smiling. 'You — you understand — Dicky — old thing; definitely.'

'Absolutely,' he told her, without smiling. 'You never were as bad as you liked to think, were you, Mercia?'

She shook her head; said: 'I was — pretty — bad. But — but now — can you — forgive me — think of me, sometimes?'

He pressed her hand; she whispered: 'Hold me tightly, Dicky — tighter . . . please . . . ' She smiled: 'That's the least you can do — for — for your — intended — wife.'

He tightened his arm about her waist. The police were silent.

Her eyes closed; her head fell back.

He stood up, and his own features were sad. Craig said: 'You were fond of her, Mr. Glenning?'

'I can't say just how I felt. She was a peculiar woman. But I won't forget her, Inspector.'

He nodded: 'There's a lot of good in even the worst of us,' he said, solemnly. 'And she was no exception.'

He covered the dead girl, quietly, removed his hat for a moment.

Her handbag lay where it had fallen — and the wedding license she had obtained lay by her side in a pool of her own blood, where it had fallen from the open bag . . .

It was unnoticed; and gradually the blood soaked it through, until it was unrecognisable.

★ ★ ★

Richard and Sheila were married a month later; once the position had been made clear to her, she could not possibly hold anything against Richard. And she was glad his seeming betrayal had been an act, an act put on only for her sake.

There was the question of settling down; and Richard put this to her.

'I shouldn't like to live in London — not after all that's happened here, Richard,' she shuddered 'I'd — I'd like to go back to mother's home at Budleigh Salterton . . . '

So Budleigh Salterton it was.

They were happy there, with each other; and if Sheila knew he carried a small photograph of Mercia Standard, always in the back of his wallet, she was wise enough to say nothing about it.

We do hope that you have enjoyed reading this large print book.

Did you know that all of our titles are available for purchase?

We publish a wide range of high quality large print books including:
Romances, Mysteries, Classics
General Fiction
Non Fiction and Westerns

Special interest titles available in large print are:
The Little Oxford Dictionary
Music Book, Song Book
Hymn Book, Service Book

Also available from us courtesy of Oxford University Press:
Young Readers' Dictionary
(large print edition)
Young Readers' Thesaurus
(large print edition)

For further information or a free brochure, please contact us at:
Ulverscroft Large Print Books Ltd.,
The Green, Bradgate Road, Anstey,
Leicester, LE7 7FU, England.
Tel: (00 44) **0116 236 4325**
Fax: (00 44) **0116 234 0205**